"I want my chil... We'll marry as soon... arrange it."

Sabrina pulled out of his hold as if his hands had burned her. "You don't have to be so old-fashioned about it, Max. I'm not asking you to marry me."

"I'm not asking you. I'm telling you what's going to happen." As proposals went, Max knew it wasn't flashy. He'd proposed in a past life and he had sworn he would never do it again. But this was different. This was about duty and responsibility, not foolish, fleeting, fickle feelings. "We will marry next month."

"Next month?" Her eyes rounded in shock. "Are you crazy? This is the twenty-first century. Couples don't have to marry because they happened to get pregnant."

"Do you really think I would walk away from the responsibility to my own flesh and blood? We will marry, and that's final."

One Night With Consequences

When one night...leads to pregnancy!

When succumbing to a night of unbridled desire, it's impossible to think past the morning after!

But with the sheets barely settled, that little blue line appears on the pregnancy test, and it doesn't take long to realize that one night of white-hot passion has turned into a lifetime of consequences!

Only one question remains:

How do you tell a man you've just met that you're about to share more than just his bed?

Find out in:

Look for more One Night With Consequences coming soon!

Melanie Milburne

THE VENETIAN ONE-NIGHT BABY

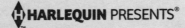

Recycling programs
for this product may
not exist in your area.

ISBN-13: 978-1-335-47803-0

The Venetian One-Night Baby

First North American publication 2019

Copyright © 2019 by Melanie Milburne

Printed in U.S.A.

www.Harlequin.com

Melanie Milburne read her first Harlequin novel at the age of seventeen, in between studying for her final exams. After completing a master's degree in education, she decided to write a novel, and thus her career as a romance author was born. Melanie is an ambassador for the Australian Childhood Foundation and a keen dog lover and trainer. She enjoys long walks in the Tasmanian bush. In 2015 Melanie won the HOLT Medallion, a prestigious award honoring outstanding literary talent.

Books by Melanie Milburne

Harlequin Presents

The Tycoon's Marriage Deal
A Virgin for a Vow
Blackmailed into the Marriage Bed
Tycoon's Forbidden Cinderella

Conveniently Wed!

Bound by a One-Night Vow

One Night With Consequences

A Ring for the Greek's Baby

The Ravensdale Scandals

Ravensdale's Defiant Captive
Awakening the Ravensdale Heiress
Engaged to Her Ravensdale Enemy
The Most Scandalous Ravensdale

The Scandal Before the Wedding

Claimed for the Billionaire's Convenience

Visit the Author Profile page
at Harlequin.com for more titles.

To Mallory (Mal) and Mike Tuffy. It was so lovely to meet you on the European river cruise a few years ago—it must be time for another one! It's wonderful to continue our friendship since. We always look forward to seeing you in Tasmania.
Xxx

CHAPTER ONE

SABRINA WAS HOPING she wouldn't run into Max Firbank again after The Kiss. He wasn't an easy man to avoid since he was her parents' favourite godson and was invited to just about every Midhurst family gathering. Birthdays, Christmas, New Year's Eve, parties and anniversaries he would spend on the fringes of the room, a twenty-first-century reincarnation of Jane Austen's taciturn Mr Darcy. He'd look down his aristocratic nose at everyone else having fun.

Sabrina made sure she had extra fun just to annoy him. She danced with everyone who asked her, chatting and working the room like she was the star student from Social Butterfly School. Max occasionally wouldn't show, and then she would spend the whole evening wondering why the energy in the room wasn't the same. But she refused to acknowledge it had anything to do with his absence.

This weekend she was in Venice to exhibit two of her designs at her first wedding expo. She felt safe from running into him—or she would have if the hotel receptionist could find her booking.

Sabrina leaned closer to the hotel reception counter. 'I can assure you the reservation was made weeks ago.'

'What name did you say it was booked under?' the young male receptionist asked.

'Midhurst, Sabrina Jane. My assistant booked it for me.'

'Do you have any documentation with you? The confirmation email?'

Had her new assistant Harriet forwarded it to her? Sabrina remembered printing out the wedding expo programme but had she printed out the accommodation details? She searched for it in her tote bag, sweat beading between her breasts, her stomach pitching with panic. She couldn't turn up flustered to her first wedding expo as an exhibitor. That's why she'd recently employed an assistant to help her with this sort of stuff. Booking flights and accommodation, sorting out her diary, making sure she didn't double book or miss appointments.

Sabrina put her lipgloss, paper diary, passport and phone on the counter, plus three pens, a small packet of tissues, some breath mints and her brand-new business cards. She left her tampons in the side pocket of her bag—there was only so much embarrassment she could handle at any one time. The only bits of paper she found were a shopping list and a receipt from her favourite shoe store.

She began to put all the items back in her bag, but her lipgloss fell off the counter, dropped to the floor, rolled across the lobby and was stopped by a large Italian-leather-clad foot.

Sabrina's gaze travelled up the long length of the expertly tailored charcoal-grey trousers and finally came to rest on Max Firbank's smoky grey-blue gaze.

'Sabrina.' His tone was less of a greeting and more of a grim *not you again*.

Sabrina gave him a tight, no-teeth-showing smile. 'Fancy seeing you here. I wouldn't have thought wedding expos were your thing.'

His eyes glanced at her mouth and something in her stomach dropped like a book tumbling off a shelf. *Kerplunk*. He blinked as if to clear his vision and bent down to pick up her lipgloss. He handed it to her, his expression as unreadable as cryptic code. 'I'm seeing a client about a project. I always stay at this hotel when I come to Venice.'

Sabrina took the lipgloss and slipped it into her bag, trying to ignore the tingling in her fingers where his had touched hers. She could feel the heat storming into her cheeks in a hot crimson tide. What sort of weird coincidence was *this*? Of all the hotels in Venice why did he have to be at *this* one? And on *this* weekend? She narrowed her gaze to the size of buttonholes. 'Did my parents tell you I was going to be here this weekend?'

Nothing on his face changed except for a brief elevation of one of his dark eyebrows. 'No. Did mine tell you I was going to be in Venice?'

Sabrina raised her chin. 'Oh, didn't you know? I zone out when your parents tell me things about you. I mentally plug my ears and sing *la-de-da* in my head until they change the subject of how amazingly brilliant you are.'

There was a flicker of movement across his lips that could have been loosely described as a smile. 'I'll have to remember to do that next time your parents bang on about you to me.'

Sabrina flicked a wayward strand of hair out of her face. Why did she always have to look like she'd been through a wind tunnel whenever she saw him? She dared not look at his mouth but kept her eyes trained on his inscrutable gaze. Was he thinking about The Kiss? The clashing of mouths that had morphed into a passionate explosion that had made a mockery of every other kiss she'd ever received? Could he still recall the taste and texture of her mouth? Did he lie in bed at night and fantasise about kissing her again?

And not just kissing, but...

'Signorina?' The hotel receptionist jolted Sabrina out of her reverie. 'We have no booking

under the name Midhurst. Could it have been another hotel you selected online?'

Sabrina suppressed a frustrated sigh. 'No. I asked my assistant to book me into this one. This is where the fashion show is being held. I have to stay here.'

'What's the problem?' Max asked in a calm, *leave it to me* tone.

Sabrina turned to face him. 'I've got a new assistant and somehow she must've got the booking wrong or it didn't process or something.' She bit her lip, trying to stem the panic punching against her heart. *Poomf. Poomf. Poomf.*

'I can put you on the cancellation list, but we're busy at this time of year so I can't guarantee anything,' the receptionist said.

Sabrina's hand crept up to her mouth and she started nibbling on her thumbnail. Too bad about her new manicure. A bit of nail chewing was all she had to soothe her rising dread. She wanted to be settled into her hotel, not left waiting on standby. What if no other hotel could take her? She needed to be close to the convention venue because she had two dresses in the fashion parade. This was her big break to get her designs on the international stage.

She. Could. Not. Fail.

'Miss Midhurst will be joining me,' Max said.

'Have the concierge bring her luggage to my room. Thank you.'

Sabrina's gaze flew to his. 'What?'

Max handed her a card key, his expression still as inscrutable as that of an MI5 spy. 'I checked in this morning. There are two beds in my suite. I only need one.'

She did *not* want to think about him and a bed in the same sentence. She'd spent the last three weeks thinking about him in a bed with her in a tangle of sweaty sex-sated limbs. Which was frankly kind of weird because she'd spent most of her life deliberately *not* thinking about him. Max was her parents' godson and almost from the moment when she'd been born six years later and become his parents' adored goddaughter, both sets of parents had decided how perfect they were for each other. It was the long-wished-for dream of both families that Max and Sabrina would fall in love, get married and have gorgeous babies together.

As if. In spite of both families' hopes, Sabrina had never got on with Max. She found him brooding and distant and arrogant. And he made it no secret he found her equally annoying…which kind of made her wonder why he'd kissed her…

But she was *not* going to think about The Kiss.

She glanced at the clock over Reception, another fist of panic pummelling her heart. She needed to shower and change and do her hair and makeup.

She needed to get her head in order. It wouldn't do to turn up flustered and nervous. What sort of impression would she make?

Sabrina took the key from him but her fingers brushed his and a tingle travelled from her fingers to her armpit. 'Maybe I should try and see if I can get in somewhere else...'

'What time does your convention start?'

'There's a cocktail party at six-thirty.'

Max led the way to the bank of lifts. 'I'll take you up to settle you in before I meet my client for a drink.'

Sabrina entered the brass embossed lift with him and the doors whispered shut behind them. The mirrored interior reflected Max's features from every angle. His tall and lean and athletic build. The well-cut dark brown hair with a hint of a wave. The generously lashed eyes the colour of storm clouds. The faint hollow below the cheekbones that gave him a chiselled-from-marble look that was far more attractive than it had any right to be. The aristocratic cut of nostril and upper lip, the small cleft in his chin, the square jaw that hinted at arrogance and a tendency to insist on his own way.

'Is your client female?' The question was out before Sabrina could monitor her wayward tongue.

'Yes.' His brusque one-word answer was a verbal Keep Out sign.

Sabrina had always been a little intrigued by his

love life. He had been jilted by his fiancée Lydia a few days before their wedding six years ago. He had never spoken of why his fiancée had called off the wedding but Sabrina had heard a whisper that it had been because Lydia had wanted children and he didn't. Max wasn't one to brandish his subsequent lovers about in public but she knew he had them from time to time. Now thirty-four, he was a virile man in his sexual prime. And she had tasted a hint of that potency when his mouth had come down on hers and sent her senses into a tailspin from which they had not yet recovered— if they ever would.

The lift stopped on Max's floor and he indicated for her to alight before him. She moved past him and breathed in the sharp citrus scent of his aftershave—lemon and lime and something else that was as mysterious and unknowable as his personality.

He led the way along the carpeted corridor and came to a suite that overlooked the Grand Canal. Sabrina stepped over the threshold and, pointedly ignoring the twin king-sized beds, went straight to the windows to check out the magnificent view. Even if her booking had been processed correctly, she would never have been able to afford a room such as this.

'Wow...' She breathed out a sigh of wonder. 'Venice never fails to take my breath away. The light. The colours. The history.' She turned to face him, doing her best to not glance at the beds that dominated the room. He still had his spy face on but she could sense an inner tension in the way he held himself. 'Erm… I'd appreciate it if you didn't tell anyone about this…'

The mocking arch of his eyebrow made her cheeks burn. 'This?'

At this rate, she'd have to ramp up the air-conditioning to counter the heat she was giving off from her burning cheeks. 'Me…sharing your room.'

'I wouldn't dream of it.'

'I mean, it could get really embarrassing if either of our parents thought we were—'

'We're not.' The blunt edge to his voice was a slap down to her ego.

There was a knock at the door.

Max opened the door and stepped aside as the hotel employee brought in Sabrina's luggage. Max gave the young man a tip and closed the door, locking his gaze on hers. 'Don't even think about it.'

Sabrina raised her eyebrows so high she thought they would fly off her face. 'You think I'm attracted to *you*? Dream on, buddy.'

The edge of his mouth lifted—the closest he got to a smile, or at least one he'd ever sent her way. 'I could have had you that night three weeks ago and you damn well know it.'

'*Had* me?' She glared at him. 'That kiss was…
was a knee-jerk thing. It just…erm…happened.
And you gave me stubble rash. I had to put on
cover-up for a week.'

His eyes went to her mouth as if he was remembering the explosive passion they'd shared. He
drew in an uneven breath and sent a hand through
the thick pelt of his hair, a frown pulling at his
forehead. 'I'm sorry. It wasn't my intention to hurt
you.' His voice had a deep gravelly edge she'd
never heard in it before.

Sabrina folded her arms. She wasn't ready to
forgive him. She wasn't ready to forgive herself
for responding to him. She wasn't ready to admit
how much she'd enjoyed that kiss and how she had
encouraged it by grabbing the front of his shirt and
pulling his head down. Argh. Why had she done
that? Neither was she ready to admit how much
she wanted him to kiss her again. 'I can think of
no one I would less like to "have me".'

Even repeating the coarse words he'd used
turned her on. Damn him. She couldn't stop thinking about what it would be like to be *had by him*.
Her sex life was practically non-existent. The only
sex she'd had in the last few years had been with
herself and even that hadn't been all that spectacu-
lar. She kept hoping she'd find the perfect partner
to help her with her issues with physical intimacy
but so far no such luck. She rarely dated anyone

more than two or three times before she decided having sex with them was out of the question. Her first and only experience of sex at the age of eighteen—*had it really been ten years ago?*—had been an ego-smashing disappointment, one she was in no hurry to repeat.

'Good. Because we're not going there,' Max said.

Sabrina inched up her chin. 'You were the one who kissed me first that night. I might have returned the kiss but only because I got caught off guard.' It was big fat lie but no way was she going to admit it. Every non-verbal signal in her repertoire had been on duty that night all but begging him to kiss her. And when he finally had, she even recalled moaning at one point. Yes, moaning with pleasure as his lips and tongue had worked their magic. *Geez*. How was she going to live *that* down?

His eyes pulsed with something she couldn't quite identify. Suppressed anger or locked-down lust or both? 'You were spoiling for a fight all through that dinner party and during the trip when I gave you a lift home.'

'So? We always argue. It doesn't mean I want you to kiss me.'

His eyes held hers in a smouldering lock that made the backs of her knees fizz. 'Are we arguing now?' His tone had a silky edge that played havoc with her senses.

Sabrina took a step back, one of her hands coming up her neck where her heart was beating like a panicked pigeon stuck in a pipe. 'I need to get ready for the c-cocktail party...' Why, oh, why did she have to sound so breathless?

He gave a soft rumble of a laugh. 'Your virtue is safe, Sabrina.' He walked to the door of the suite and turned to look at her again. 'Don't wait up. I'll be late.'

Sabrina gave him a haughty look that would have done a Regency spinster proud. 'Going to *have* your client, are you?'

He left without another word, which, annoyingly, left her with the painful echo of hers.

Max closed the door of his suite and let out a breath. Why had he done the knight in shining armour thing? Why should he care if she couldn't get herself organised enough to book a damn hotel? She would have found somewhere to stay, surely. But no. He had to do the decent thing. Nothing about how he felt about Sabrina was decent—especially after that kiss. He'd lost count of how many women he'd kissed. He wasn't a man whore, but he enjoyed sex for the physical release it gave.

But he couldn't get *that* kiss out of his mind.

Max had always avoided Sabrina in the past.

He hadn't wanted to encourage his and her parents from their sick little fantasy of them getting it on. He got it on with women he chose and he made sure his choices were simple and straightforward—sex without strings.

Sabrina was off limits because she was the poster girl for the happily-ever-after fairytale. She was looking for Mr Right to sweep her off her feet and park her behind a white picket fence with a double pram with a couple of chubby-cheeked progeny tucked inside.

Max had nothing against marriage, but he no longer wanted it for himself. Six years ago, his fiancée had called off their wedding, informing him she had fallen in love with someone else, with someone who wanted children—the children Max refused to give her. Prior to that, Lydia had been adamant she was fine with his decision not to have kids. He'd thought everything was ticking along well enough in their relationship. He'd been more annoyed than upset at Lydia calling off their relationship. It had irritated him that he hadn't seen it coming.

But it had taught him a valuable lesson. A lesson he was determined he would never have to learn again. He wasn't cut out for long-term relationships. He didn't have what it took to handle commitment and all its responsibilities.

He knew marriage worked for some people—

his parents and Sabrina's had solid relationships that had been tried and tested and triumphed over tragedy, especially his parents. The loss of his baby brother Daniel at the age of four months had devastated them, of course.

Max had been seven years old and while his parents had done all they could to shield him from the tragedy, he still carried his share of guilt. In spite of the coroner's verdict of Sudden Infant Death Syndrome, Max could never get it out of his mind that he had been the last person to see his baby brother alive. There wasn't a day that went by when he didn't think of his brother, of all the years Daniel had missed out on. The milestones he would never meet.

Max walked out of his hotel and followed the Grand Canal, almost oblivious to the crowds of tourists that flocked to Venice at this time of year. Whenever he thought of Daniel, a tiny worm of guilt burrowed its way into his mind. Was there something he could have done to save his brother? Why hadn't he noticed something? Why hadn't he checked him more thoroughly? The lingering guilt he felt about Daniel was something he was almost used to now. He was almost used to feeling the lurch of dread in his gut whenever he saw a small baby. Almost.

Max stepped out of the way of a laughing couple that were walking arm in arm, carrying the colourful Venetian masks they'd bought from one of the many vendors along the canal. Why hadn't he thought to book a room at another hotel for Sabrina? It wasn't as if he couldn't afford it. He'd made plenty of money as a world-acclaimed architect, and he knew things were a little tight with her financially as she was still building up her wedding-dress design business and stubbornly refusing any help from her doctor parents, who had made it no secret that they would have preferred her to study medicine like them and Sabrina's two older brothers.

Had he *wanted* her in his room? Had he instinctively seized at the chance to have her to himself so he could kiss her again?

Maybe do more than kiss her?

Max pulled away from the thought like he was stepping back from a too-hot fire. But that's exactly what Sabrina was—hot. Too hot. She made him hot and bothered and horny as hell. The way she picked fights with him just to get under his skin never failed to get his blood pumping. Her cornflower-blue eyes would flash and sparkle, and her soft and supple mouth would fling cutting retorts his way, and it would make him feel alive in a way he hadn't in years.

Alive and energised.

But no. No. No. No. No.

He must *not* think about Sabrina like that. He

had to keep his distance. He had to. She wasn't the sex without strings type. She wasn't a fling girl; she was a fairytale girl. And she was his parents' idea of his ideal match—his soul mate or something. Nothing against his parents, but they were wrong. Dead wrong. Sabrina was spontaneous and creative and disorganised. He was logical, responsible and organised to the point of pedantic. How could anyone think they were an ideal couple? It was crazy. He only had to spend a few minutes with her and she drove him nuts.

How was he going to get through a whole weekend with her?

CHAPTER TWO

SABRINA WAS A little late getting to the cocktail party, which was being held in a private room at the hotel. Only the designers and models and their agents and select members of the press were invited. She entered the party room with her stomach in a squirming nest of nibbling and nipping nerves. Everyone looked glamorous and sophisticated. She was wearing a velvet dress she'd made herself the same shade of blue as her eyes and had scooped her hair up into a bun and paid extra attention to her makeup—hence why she was late to the party.

A waiter came past with a tray of drinks and Sabrina took a glass of champagne and took a generous sip to settle her nerves. She wasn't good at networking...well, not unless she was showing off in front of Max. She always worried she might say the wrong thing or make a social faux pas that would make everyone snigger at her.

Large gatherings reminded her of the school

formal the day after she'd slept with her boyfriend for the first time. The rumourmongers had been at work, fuelled by the soul-destroying text messages her boyfriend had sent to all his mates. Sabrina had heard each cruelly taunting comment, seen every mocking look cast in her direction from people she had thought were her friends.

She had stood behind a column in the venue to try and escape the shameful whispers and had heard her boyfriend tell a couple of his mates what a frigid lay she had been. The overwhelming sense of shame had been crippling. Crucifying.

Sabrina sipped some more champagne and fixed a smile on her face. She had to keep her head and not time-travel. She wasn't eighteen any more. She was twenty-eight and ran her own business, for pity's sake. She. Could. Do. This.

'You're Sabrina Midhurst, aren't you?' a female member of the press said, smiling. 'I recognised you from the expo programme photo. You did a friend's wedding dress. It was stunning.'

'Yes, that's me,' Sabrina said, smiling back. 'And I'm glad you liked your friend's dress.'

'I'd like to do a feature article on you.' The woman handed Sabrina a card with her name and contact details on it. 'I'm Naomi Nettleton, I'm a freelancer but I've done articles for some big-name fashion magazines. There's a lot of interest in your work. Would you be interested in giving me an interview? Maybe we could grab a few minutes after this?'

Sabrina could barely believe her ears. An interview in a glossy magazine? That sort of exposure was gold dust. Her Love Is in the Care boutique in London was small and she'd always dreamed of expanding. She and her best friend Holly Frost, who was a wedding florist, hoped to set up their shops side by side in Bloomsbury in order to boost each other's trade. At the moment, they were blocks away from each other but Sabrina knew it would be a brilliant business move if they could pull it off.

She wanted to prove to her doctor parents the creative path she'd chosen to follow wasn't just a whim but a viable business venture. She came from a long line of medicos. Her parents, her grandparents and both her brothers were all in the medical profession. But she had never wanted that for herself. She would much rather have a tape measure around her neck than a stethoscope.

She had been drawing wedding gowns since she was five years old. All through her childhood she had made dresses out of scraps of fabric. She had dressed every doll and teddy bear or soft toy she'd possessed in wedding finery. All through her teens she had collected scrapbooks with hundreds of sketches and cuttings from magazines. She'd had to withstand considerable family pressure in order to pursue her dream and success was her way of proving she had made the right choice.

Sabrina arranged to meet the journalist in the bar downstairs after the party. She continued to circulate, speaking with the models who had been chosen to wear her designs and also with the fashion parade manager who had personally invited her to the event after her daughter had bought one of Sabrina's designs.

She took another glass of champagne off a passing waiter.

Who said word of mouth didn't still work?

Max came back to the hotel after the dinner with his client had gone on much later than he'd originally planned. He hadn't intended having more than a drink with Loretta Barossi but had ended up lingering over a meal with her because he hadn't wanted to come back to his room before Sabrina was safely tucked up and, hopefully, asleep in bed. Unfortunately, he'd somehow given the thirty-six-year-old recently divorced woman the impression he'd been enjoying her company far more than he had, and then had to find a way to politely reject her broadly hinted invitation to spend the night with her. But that was another line he never crossed—mixing business with pleasure.

He was walking past the bar situated off the lobby when he saw Sabrina sitting on one of the plush sofas talking to a woman and a man who was holding a camera in his lap. As if she sensed his presence, Sabrina turned her glossy honey-brown head and saw him looking at her. She raised her hand and gave him a surreptitious fingertip wave and the woman with her glanced to see to whom she was waving. The woman leaned forward to say something to Sabrina, and even from this distance Max could see the rush of a blush flooding Sabrina's creamy cheeks.

He figured the less people who saw him with Sabrina the better, but somehow he found himself walking towards her before he could stop himself. What had the other woman said to make Sabrina colour up like that?

Sabrina's eyes widened when he approached their little party and she reached for her glass of champagne and promptly knocked it over. 'Oops. Sorry. I—'

'You're Max Firbank, the award-winning architect,' the young woman said, rising to offer her hand. 'I've seen an article about your work in one of the magazines I worked for a couple of years ago. When Sabrina said she was sharing a room with a friend, I didn't realise she was referring to you.' Her eyebrows suggestively rose over the word *friend*.

Sabrina had stopped trying to mop up her drink with a paper napkin and stood, clutching the wet and screwed-up napkin in her hand. 'Oh, he's not *that* sort of friend,' she said with a choked little laugh. 'I had a problem with my booking and Max offered me his bed, I mean *a* bed. He has two. Two big ones—they look bigger than king-sized, you could fit a dozen people in each. It's a huge room, so much space we hardly know the other is there, isn't that right, Max?' She turned her head to look at him and he almost had to call for a fire extinguisher because her cheeks were so fiery red.

Max wasn't sure why he slipped his arm around her slim waist and drew her to his body. Maybe it was because she was kind of cute when she got flustered and he liked being able to get under her skin for a change, the way she got under his. Besides, he didn't know any other woman he could make blush more than her. And, yes, he got a kick out of touching her, especially after That Kiss, which she enjoyed as much as he had, even though she was intent on denying it. 'You don't have to be shy about our relationship, baby.' He flashed one of his rare smiles. 'We're both consenting adults.'

'Aw, don't you make a gorgeous couple?' the woman said. 'Tim, get a photo of them,' she said to the man holding the camera. 'I'll include it in the article about Sabrina's designs. That is, if you don't have any objection?'

Hell, yeah. He had one big objection. He didn't mind teasing a blush or two out of Sabrina but if his family got a whiff of him sharing a room with her in Venice they would be measuring him for a morning suit and booking the church. Max held up his hand like a stop sign. 'Sorry. I don't make a habit of broadcasting my private life in the press.'

The woman sighed and handed him a business card. 'Here are my details if you change your mind.'

'I won't.' He gave both the journalist and the photographer a polite nod and added, 'It was nice meeting you. If you'll excuse us? It's been a big day for Sabrina. She needs her beauty sleep.'

Sabrina followed Max to the lift but there were other people waiting to use it as well so she wasn't able to vent her spleen. What was he thinking? She'd been trying to play down her relationship with Max to the journalist, but he'd given Naomi Nettleton the impression they were an item. She stood beside him in the lift as it stopped and started as it delivered guests to their floors.

Max stood calmly beside her with his expression in its customary inscrutable lines, although she sensed there was a mocking smile lurking behind the screen of his gaze. She moved closer to him to allow another guest into the lift on level ten and placed her high heel on Max's foot and pressed down with all her weight. He made a grunting sound that sounded far sexier than she'd expected and he placed the iron band of his arm around her middle and drew her back against him so her back was flush against his pelvis.

Her mind swam with images of them locked together in a tangle of sweaty limbs, his body driving into hers. Even now she could feel the swell of his body, the rush of blood that told her he was as aroused as she was. Her breathing quickened, her legs weakened, her heart rate rocketed. The steely strength of his arm lying across her stomach was burning a brand into her flesh. Her inner core tensed, the electric heat of awakened desire coursing through her in pulses and flickers.

The mirrors surrounding them reflected their intimate clinch from a thousand angles but Sabrina wasn't prepared to make a scene in front of the other guests, one of whom she had seen at the cocktail party. After all, she had a professional image to uphold and slapping Max's face—if indeed she was the sort of person to inflict violence on another person—was not the best way to maintain it.

But, oh, how she longed to slap both his cheeks until they were as red as hers. Then she would elbow him in the ribs and stomp on his toes. Then she would rip the clothes from his body, score her fingernails down his chest and down his back until he begged for mercy. But wait...why was she thinking of ripping his clothes off his body?

No. No. No. She must not think about Max without clothes. She must not think about him naked.

She. Must. Not.

Max unlocked the door and she brushed past him and almost before he had time to close it she let fly. 'What the hell were you playing at down there? You gave the impression we were sleeping together. What's *wrong* with you? You know how much I hate you. Why did you—?'

'You don't hate me.' His voice was so calm it made hers sound all the more irrational and childish.

'If I didn't before, I do now.' Sabrina poked him in the chest. 'What was all that about in the lift?'

He captured her by the waist and brought her closer, hip to hip, his eyes more blue than grey and glinting with something that made her belly turn over. 'You know exactly what it was about. And just like that kiss, you enjoyed every second of it. Deny it if you dare.'

Sabrina intended to push away from him but somehow her hands grabbed the front of his jacket instead. He smelt like sun-warmed lemons and her senses were as intoxicated as if she had breathed in a potent aroma. An aroma that made her forget how much she hated him and instead made her want him with every throbbing traitorous cell of her body. Or maybe she was tipsy from all the champagne she'd had downstairs at the party and in the bar. It was making her drop her inhibitions. Sabotaging her already flagging self-control. Her head was spinning a little but didn't it always when he looked at her like that?

His mouth was tilted in a cynical slant, the dark stubble around his nose and mouth more obvious now than earlier that evening. It gave him a rakish air that was strangely attractive. Dangerously, deliciously attractive. She was acutely aware of every point of contact with his body: her hips, her breasts and her belly where his belt buckle was pressing.

And not just his belt buckle, but the proud surge of his male flesh—a heady reminder of the lust that simmered and boiled and blistered between them.

The floor began to shift beneath her feet and Sabrina's hands tightened on his jacket. The room was moving, pitching like a boat tossed about on a turbulent ocean. Her head felt woolly, her thoughts trying to push through the fog like a hand fumbling for a light switch in the dark. But then a sudden wave of nausea assailed her and she swayed and would have toppled backwards if Max hadn't countered it with a firm hand at her back.

'Are you okay?' His voice had a note of concern but it came from a long way off as if he was speaking to her through a long vacuum.

She was vaguely aware of his other hand coming to grasp her by the shoulder to stabilise her, but then her vision blurred and her stomach contents threatened mutiny. She made a choking sound and pushed Max back and stumbled towards the bathroom.

To her mortifying shame, Max witnessed the whole of the undignified episode. But she was beyond caring. And besides, it had been quite comforting to have her hair held back from her face and to have the soft press of a cool facecloth on the back of her neck.

Sabrina sat back on her heels when the worst of it was over. Her head was pounding and her stomach felt as it if had been scraped with a sharp-edged spoon and then rinsed out with hydrochloric acid.

He handed her a fresh facecloth, his expression wry. 'Clearly I need some work on my seduction routine.'

Sabrina managed a fleeting smile. 'Funny haha.' She dragged herself up from the floor with considerable help from him, his hands warm and steady and impossibly strong. 'Argh. I should never drink on an empty stomach.'

'Wasn't there any food at the cocktail party?'

'I got there late.' She turned to inspect her reflection in the bathroom mirror and then wished she hadn't. Could she look any worse? She could almost guarantee none of the super-sophisticated women he dated ever disgraced themselves by heaving over the toilet bowl. She turned back around. 'Sorry you had to witness that.'

'You need to drink some water. Lots of it, otherwise you're going to have one hell of a hangover in the morning.' His frown and stern tone reminded her of a parent lecturing a binge-drinking teenager.

'I don't normally drink much but I was nervous.'

His frown deepened and he reached for a glass on the bathroom counter and filled it from the tap and then handed it to her. 'Is this a big deal for you? This wedding expo?'

Sabrina took the glass from him and took a couple of sips to see how her stomach coped. 'It's the first time I've been invited to exhibit some of my designs. It's huge for me. It can take new designers years to get noticed but luckily the fashion show floor manager's daughter bought one of my dresses and she liked it so much she invited me along. And then Naomi, the journalist in the bar, asked for an interview for a feature article. It's a big opportunity for me to get my name out there, especially in Europe.' She drained the glass of water and handed it back to him.

He dutifully refilled it and handed it back, his frown still carving a trench between his brows. 'What did you tell her about us?'

'Nothing. I didn't even mention your name. I just said I was sharing a room with a friend.'

'Are you sure you didn't mention me?'

Sabrina frowned. 'Why would I link my name with yours? Do you think I want anyone back home to know we're sharing a room? Give me a break. I'm not *that* stupid. If I let that become common knowledge our parents will have wedding invitations in the post before you can blink.' She took a breath and continued, 'Anyway, you were the one who made it look like we were having a dirty weekend. You called me "baby", for God's sake.'

'Drink your water,' he said as if she hadn't spoken. 'You need to get some rest if you want to look your best for tomorrow.'

Sabrina scowled at him over the top of her glass. 'Do you have to remind me I look a frightful mess?'

He released a slow breath. 'I'll see you in the morning. Goodnight.'

When Sabrina came out of the bathroom after a shower there was no sign of him in the suite. She wondered if he'd left to give her some privacy or whether he had other plans. Why should she care if he hooked up with someone for a night of unbridled passion? She pulled down the covers on one of the beds and slipped between the cool and silky sheets and closed her eyes...

* * *

Max went for a long walk through the streets and alleys of Venice to clear his head. He could still feel the imprint of Sabrina's body pressing against him in the lift. He'd been hard within seconds. His fault for holding her like that, but the temptation had caught him off guard. Had it been his imagination or had she leaned back into him?

He wanted her.

He hated admitting it. Loathed admitting it but there it was. He was in lust with her. He couldn't remember when he'd started noticing her in that way. It had crept up on him over the last few months. The way his body responded when she looked at him in a certain way. The way his blood surged when she stood up to him and flashed her blue eyes at him in defiance. The way she moved her dancer-slim body making him fantasise about how she would look naked.

He had to get over it. Ignore it or something. Having a fling with Sabrina would hurt too many people. Hadn't he hurt his parents enough? If he started a fling with her everyone would get their hopes up that it would become permanent.

He didn't do permanent.

He would get his self-control back in line and get through the weekend without touching her. He opened and closed his hands, trying to rid himself of the feeling of her soft skin. Trying to remove the sensation of her touch. What was wrong with him? Why couldn't he just ignore her the way he had for most of his adult life? He'd always kept his distance. Always. He avoided speaking with her. He had watched from the sidelines as she'd spoken to everyone at the various gatherings they'd both attended.

There was no way a relationship between them would work. Not even a short-term one. She had fairytale written all over her. She came from a family of doctors and yet she had resisted following the tradition and become a wedding-dress designer instead. Didn't that prove how obsessed with the fairytale she was?

His mistake had been kissing her three weeks ago. He didn't understand how he had gone from arguing with her over something to finding her pulling his head down and then his mouth coming down on hers and… He let out a shuddering breath. Why was he *still* thinking about that damn kiss? The heat of their mouths connecting had tilted the world on its axis, or at least it had felt like it at the time. He could have sworn the floor had shifted beneath his feet. If he closed his eyes he could still taste her sweetness, could still feel the soft pliable texture of her lips moving against his, could still feel the sexy dart of her tongue.

The worst of it was he had lost control. Desire had swept through him and he still didn't know how he'd stopped himself from taking her then and there. And *that* scared the hell of out him.

It would not—*could* not—happen again.

When Max entered the suite in the early hours of the morning, Sabrina was sound asleep, curled up like a kitten, her brown hair spilling over the pillow. One of her hands was tucked under the cheek; the other was lying on the top of the covers. She was wearing a cream satin nightie for he could see the delicate lace trim across her décolletage peeking out from where the sheet was lying across her chest.

The desire to slip into that bed and pull her into his arms was so strong he had to clench his hands into fists. He clearly had to do something about his sex life if he was ogling the one woman he wanted to avoid. When was the last time he'd been with someone? A month? Two…or was it three? He'd been busy working on multiple projects, which hadn't left much time for a social life. Not that he had a much of a social life. He preferred his own company so he could get on with his work.

Work. That's what he needed to concentrate on. He moved past the bed to go to the desk where he had set up his laptop the day before. He opened one of the accounts he was working on and started tinkering.

There was a rustle from the bed behind him

and Sabrina's drowsy voice said, 'Do you have to do that now?'

Max turned around to look at her in the muted light coming off his laptop screen. Her hair was a cloud of tangles and one of her cheeks had a linen crease and one spaghetti-thin strap of her nightie had slipped off her shoulder, revealing the upper curve of her left breast. She looked sleepy, sexy and sensual and lust hit him like a sucker punch. 'Sorry. Did I wake you?'

She pushed back some of her hair with her hand. 'Don't you *ever* sleep?'

I would if there wasn't a gorgeously sexy woman lying in the bed next to mine.

Max kept his features neutral but his body was thrumming, hardening, aching. 'How's your head? Have the construction workers started yet?'

Her mouth flickered with a sheepish smile. 'Not yet. The water helped.'

He pushed a hand through his hair and suppressed a yawn. 'Can I get you anything?'

'You don't have to wait on me, Max.' She peeled back the bed covers and swung her slim legs over the edge of the bed. She padded over to the bar fridge and opened it, the light spilling from inside a golden shaft against her long shapely legs.

'Hair of the dog?' Max injected a cautionary note in his tone.

She closed the fridge and held up a chocolate bar. 'Nope. Chocolate is the best hangover cure.'

He shrugged and turned back to his laptop. 'Whatever works, I guess.'

The sound of her unwrapping the chocolate bar was loud in the silence. Then he heard her approaching from behind, the soft *pfft, pfft, pfft* of her footsteps on the carpet reminding him of a stealthy cat. He smelt the fragrance of her perfume dance around his nostrils, the sweet peas and lilacs with an understory of honeysuckle—or was it jasmine?

'Is that one of your designs?' She was standing so close behind him every hair on the back of his neck lifted. Tensed. Tickled. Tightened.

'Yeah.'

She leaned over his shoulder, some of her hair brushing his face, and he had to call on every bit of self-control he possessed not to touch her. Her breath smelt of chocolate and temptation. In the soft light her skin had a luminous glow, the creamy perfection of her skin making him ache to run his finger down the slope of her cheek. He let out the breath he hadn't realised he'd been holding and clicked the computer mouse. 'Here. I'll give you a virtual tour.' He showed her the presentation he'd been working on for a client, trying to ignore the closeness of her body.

'Wow...' She smiled and glanced at him, her head still bent close to his. 'It's amazing.'

Max couldn't tear his eyes away from the curve of her mouth. Its plump ripeness, the top lip just as full as the lower one and the neat definition of the philtrum ridge below her nose. He met her gaze and something in the atmosphere changed. The silence so intense he was sure he could hear his blood pounding. He could certainly feel it—it was swelling his groin to a painful tightness. He put his hand down on hers where it was resting on the desk, holding it beneath the gentle but firm pressure of his. He felt her flinch as if his touch electrified her and her eyes widened into shimmering pools of cornflower blue.

The tip of her tongue swept over her lips, her breath coming out in a jagged stream. 'Max…' Her voice was whisper soft, tentative and uncertain.

He lifted her hand from the desk and toyed with her fingers, watching every micro-expression on her face. Her skin was velvet soft and he was getting off thinking about her hands stroking his body. Stroking *him*. Was she thinking about it? About the heat they generated? About the lust that swirled and simmered and sizzled between them? She kept glancing at his mouth, her throat rising and falling over a series of delicate swallows. Her breathing was uneven. He was still seated and she was standing, but because of the height ratio, he was just about at eye level with her breasts.

But the less he thought about her breasts the better.

Max released her hand and rose from the desk chair in an abrupt movement. 'Go back to bed, Sabrina.' He knew he sounded as stern as a schoolmaster but he had to get the damn genie back in the lamp. The genie of lust. The wicked genie that had been torturing him since he'd foolishly kissed Sabrina three weeks ago.

'I was sound asleep in bed before you started tapping away at your computer.' Sabrina's tone was tinged with resentment.

Max let out a long slow breath. 'I don't want to argue with you. Now go to—'

'Why don't you want to argue with me?' Her eyes flashed blue sparks. 'Because you might be tempted to kiss me again?'

He kept his expression under lockdown. 'We're not doing this, Sabrina.'

'Not doing what?' Her mouth was curved in a mocking manner. 'You were going to kiss me again, weren't you? Go on. Admit it.'

Max gave his own version of a smile and shook his head as if he was dealing with a misguided child. 'No. I was not going to kiss you.'

She straightened her shoulders and folded her arms. 'Liar.'

Max held her gaze, his body throbbing with need. No one could get him as worked up as her.

No one. Their verbal banter was a type of fore-play. When had it started to become like that? For years, their arguments had just been arguments—the clash of two strong-willed personalities. But over the last few months something had changed. Was that why he'd gone to the dinner party of a mutual friend because he'd known she'd be there? Was that why he'd offered to drive her home because her car was being serviced? There had been other people at the dinner who could have taken her but, no, he'd insisted.

He couldn't even recall what they'd been arguing about on the way home or who had started it. But he remembered all too well how it had ended and he had to do everything in his power to make sure it never happened again. 'Why would I kiss you again? You don't want another dose of stubble rash, do you?'

Her combative expression floundered for a moment and her teeth snagged her lower lip. 'Okay... so I might have been lying about that...'

Max kept his gaze trained on hers. 'You're not asking me to kiss you, are you?'

The sparkling light of defiance was back in her eyes. 'Of course not.' She gave a spluttering laugh as if the idea was ludicrous. 'I would rather kiss a cane toad.'

'Good.' He slammed his lips shut on the word. 'Better keep it that way.'

CHAPTER THREE

SABRINA STALKED BACK to her bed, climbed in and pulled the covers up to her chin. Of course she'd wanted Max to kiss her. And she was positive he'd wanted to kiss her too. It secretly thrilled her that he found her so attractive. Why wouldn't it thrill her? She had all the usual female needs and she hadn't made love with a man since she was eighteen.

Not that what had happened back then could be called, by any stretch of the imagination, making love. It had been selfish one-sided sex. She had been little more than a vessel for her boyfriend to use to satisfy his base needs. She'd naively thought their relationship had been more than that. Much more. She had thought herself in love. She hadn't wanted her first time to be with someone who didn't care about her. She had been so sure Brad loved her. He'd even told her he loved her. But as soon as the deed was done he was gone. He'd dumped her and called her horrible names to his friends that still made her cringe and curl up in shame.

Sabrina heard Max preparing for bed. He went into the bathroom and brushed his teeth, coming out a few minutes later dressed in one of the hotel bathrobes. Was he naked under that robe? Her mind raced with images of his tanned and toned flesh, her body tingling at the thought of lying pinned beneath him in the throes of sizzling hot sex.

She couldn't imagine Max ever leaving a lover unsatisfied. He only had to look at her and she was halfway to an orgasm. It was embarrassing how much she wanted him. It was like lust had hijacked her body, turning her into a wanton woman who could think of nothing but earthly pleasures. Even now her body felt restless, every nerve taut with the need for touch. *His* touch. Was it possible to hate someone and want them at the same time? Or was there something wrong with her? Why was she so fiercely attracted to someone she could barely conduct a civil conversation with without it turning into a blistering argument?

But why *did* they always argue?

And why did she find it so...so stimulating?

It was a little lowering to realise how much she enjoyed their verbal spats. She looked forward to them. She got secretly excited when she knew he was going to be at a function she would be attending, even though she pretended otherwise to her family. No wonder she found joint family functions deadly boring if he didn't show up. Did she have some sort of disorder? Did she crave negative interaction with him because it was the only way she could get him to notice her?

Sabrina closed her eyes when Max walked past her bed, every pore of her body aware of him. She heard the sheets being pulled back and the sound of him slipping between them. She heard the click of the bedside lamp being switched off and then he let out a sigh that sounded bone-weary.

'I hope you don't snore.' The comment was out before she could stop herself.

He gave a sound that might have been a muttered curse but she couldn't quite tell. 'No one's complained so far.'

A silence ticked, ticked, ticked like an invisible clock.

'I probably should warn you I've been known to sleepwalk,' Sabrina said.

'I knew that. Your mother told me.'

She turned over so she was facing his bed. There was enough soft light coming in through the gap in the curtains for her to see him. He was lying on his back with his eyes closed, the sheets pulled to the level of his waist, the gloriously naked musculature of his chest making her mouth water. He looked like a sexy advertisement for luxury bed linen. His tanned skin a stark contrast to the white sheets. 'When did she tell you?'

'Years ago.'

Sabrina propped herself up on one elbow. 'How many years ago?'

He turned his head in her direction and opened one eye. 'I don't remember. What does it matter?'

She plucked at the sheet covering her breasts. What else had her mother told him about her? 'I don't like the thought of her discussing my private details with you.'

He closed his eye and turned his head back to lie flat on the pillow. 'Bit late for that, sweetheart.' His tone was so dry it could have soaked up an oil spill. 'Your parents have been citing your considerable assets to me ever since you hit puberty.'

Sabrina could feel her cheeks heating. She knew exactly how pushy her parents had been. But so too had his parents. Both families had engineered situations where she and Max would be forced together, especially since his fiancée Lydia had broken up with him just before their wedding six years ago. She even wondered if the family pressure had actually scared poor Lydia off. What woman wanted to marry a man whose parents staunchly believed she wasn't the right one for him? His parents had hardly been subtle about their hopes. It had been mildly embarrassing at first, but over the years it had become annoying. So annoying that Sabrina had stubbornly refused to acknowledge any of Max's good qualities.

And he had many now that she thought about it. He was steady in a crisis. He thought before he spoke. He was hard working and responsible and organised. He was a supremely talented architect and had won numerous awards for his designs. But she had never heard him boast about his achievements. She had only heard about them via his parents.

Sabrina lay back down with a sigh. 'Yeah, well, hate to tell you but your parents have been doing the same about you.' She kicked out the rumples in her bed linen with her feet and added, 'Anyone would think you were a saint.'

'I'm hardly that.'

There was another silence.

'Thanks for letting me share your room,' she said. 'I don't know what I would have done if you hadn't offered. I heard from other people at the cocktail party that just about everywhere else is full.'

'It's fine. Glad to help.'

She propped herself back on her elbow to look at him. 'Max?'

He made a sound that sounded like a *God, give me strength* groan. 'Mmm?'

'Why did you and Lydia break up?' Sabrina wasn't sure why she'd asked the question other than she had always wondered what had caused his fiancée to cancel their wedding at short notice. She'd heard the gossip over the children issue but she wanted to hear the truth from him.

The movement of his body against the bed linen sounded angry. And the air seemed to tighten in the room as if the walls and ceiling and the furniture had collectively taken a breath.

'Go to sleep, Sabrina.' His tone had an intractable *don't push it* edge.

Sabrina wanted to push it. She wanted to push him into revealing more about himself. There was so much she didn't know about him. There were things he never spoke about—like the death of his baby brother. But then neither did his parents speak about Daniel. The tragic loss of an infant was always devastating and even though Max had been only seven years old at the time, he too would have felt the loss, especially with his parents so distraught with grief. Sometimes she saw glimpses of his parents' grief even now. A certain look would be exchanged between Gillian and Bryce Firbank and their gazes would shadow as if they were remembering their baby boy. 'Someone told me it was because she wanted kids and you didn't. Is that true?'

He didn't answer for such a long moment she

thought he must have fallen asleep. But then she heard the sound of the sheets rustling and his voice broke through the silence. 'That and other reasons.'

'Such as?'

He released a frustrated-sounding sigh. 'She fell in love with someone else.'

'Did you love her?'

'I was going to marry her, wasn't I?' His tone had an edge of impatience that made her wonder if he had been truly in love with his ex-fiancée. He had never seemed to her to be the falling-in-love type. He was too self-contained. Too private with his emotions. Sabrina remembered meeting Lydia a couple of times and feeling a little surprised she and Max were a couple about to be married. The chemistry between them had been on the mild instead of the wild side.

'Lydia's divorced now, isn't she?' Sabrina continued after a long moment. 'I wonder if she ever thinks she made the wrong decision.'

He didn't answer but she could tell from his breathing he wasn't asleep.

Sabrina closed her eyes, willing herself to relax, but sleep was frustratingly elusive. Her body was too strung out, too aware of Max lying so close by. She listened to the sound of him breathing and the slight rustle of the sheets when he changed position. After a while his breathing slowed and the rustling stopped and she realised he was finally asleep.

She settled back down against the pillows with a sigh...

Max could hear a baby crying...the sound making his skin prickle with cold dread. Where was the baby? What was wrong with it? Why was it crying? Why wasn't anyone going to it? Should he try and settle it? Then he saw the cot, his baby brother's cot...it was empty... Then he saw the tiny white coffin with the teddy bear perched on top. *No. No. No.*

'Max. Max.' Sabrina's voice broke through the nightmare. 'You're having a bad dream. Wake up, Max. Wake up.'

Max opened his eyes and realised with a shock he was holding her upper arms in a deathly grip. She was practically straddling him, her hair tousled from being in bed or from him manhandling her. He released her and let out a juddering breath, shame and guilt coursing through him like a rush of ice water. 'I'm sorry. Did I hurt you?' He winced when he saw the full set of his fingerprints on her arms.

She rubbed her hands up and down her arms, her cheeks flushed. 'I'm okay. But you scared the hell out of me.'

Max pushed back the sheets and swung his legs

over the edge of the bed, his back facing her. He rested his hands on his thighs, trying to get his heart rate back to normal. Trying not to look at those marks on her arms. Trying not to reach for her.

Desperately trying not to reach for her.

'Max?' Her voice was as soft as the hand she laid on his shoulder.

'Go back to sleep.'

She was so close to him he could feel her breath on the back of his neck. He could feel her hair tickling his shoulder and he knew if he so much as turned his head to look at her he would be lost. It had been years since he'd had a nightmare. They weren't as frequent as in the early days but they still occasionally occurred. Catching him off guard, reminding him he would never be free from the pain of knowing he had failed his baby brother.

'Do you want to talk about your nightmare?' Sabrina said. 'It might help you to—'

'No.'

Sabrina's soft hand was moving up and down between his shoulder blades in soothing strokes. His skin lifted in a shiver, his blood surging to his groin. Her hand came up and began to massage the tight muscles of his neck and he suppressed a groan of pleasure. Why couldn't he be immune to her touch? Why couldn't he ignore the way she was leaning against him, one of her satin-covered breasts brushing against his left shoulder blade? He could smell her flowery fragrance; it teased and tantalised his senses. He felt drugged. Stoned by her closeness.

He drew in a breath and placed his hands on either side of his thighs, his fingers digging into the mattress. He would *not* touch her.

He. Would. Not.

Sabrina could feel the tension in his body. The muscles in his back and shoulders were set like concrete, even the muscles in his arms were bunched and the tendons of his hands white and prominent where he was gripping the mattress. His thrashing about his bed had woken her from a fitful sleep. She had been shocked at the sound of his anguish, his cries hadn't been all that loud but they had been raw and desperate and somehow that made them seem all the more tragic. What had he been dreaming about? And why wouldn't he talk about it? Or it had it just been one of those horrible dreams everyone had from time to time?

Sabrina moved her hand from massaging his neck to trail it through the thickness of his hair. 'You should try and get some sleep.'

'You're not helping.' His voice was hard bitten like he was spitting out each word.

She kept playing with his hair, somehow realising he was like a wounded dog, snipping and snarling at anyone who got too close. She was close. So close one of her breasts was pressing against the rock-hard plane of his shoulder blade. The contact, even through the satin of her nightie, made her breast tingle and her nipple tighten. 'Do you have nightmares often?'

'Sabrina, please…' He turned and looked at her, his eyes haunted.

She touched his jaw with the palm of her hand, gliding it down the rough stubble until she got to the cleft in his chin. She traced it with her finger and then did the same to the tight line of his mouth, exploring it in intimate detail, recalling how it felt clamped to hers. 'Do you ever think about that night? The night we kissed?' Her voice was barely more than a whisper.

He opened and closed his mouth, the lips pressing together as if he didn't trust himself to use them against hers. 'Kissing you was a mistake. I won't be repeating it.'

Sabrina frowned. 'It didn't feel like a mistake to me… It felt…amazing. The best kiss I've ever had, in fact.'

Something passed through his gaze—a flicker of heat, of longing, of self-control wavering. Then he raised a hand and gently cupped her cheek, his eyes dipping to her mouth, a shudder going through him like an aftershock. 'We shouldn't be doing this.' His voice was so gruff it sounded like he'd been gargling gravel.

'Why shouldn't we?' Sabrina leaned closer, drawn to him as if pulled by an invisible force.

He swallowed and slid his hand to the sensitive skin of her nape, his fingers tangling into her hair, sending her scalp into a tingling torrent of pleasure. 'Because it can't go anywhere.'

'Who said I wanted it to go anywhere?' Sabrina asked. 'I'm just asking you to kiss me, not marry me. You kiss other women, don't you?'

His breath came out and sent a tickling waft of air across the surface of her lips. 'The thing is… I'm not sure I can *just* kiss you.'

She stared at him in pleasant surprise. So pleasant her ego got out of the foetal position and did a victory dance. 'What are you saying?' She couldn't seem to speak louder than a whispery husk.

His eyes had a dark pulsing intensity that made her inner core contract. 'I want you. But I—'

'Can we skip the but?' Sabrina said. 'Let's go back to the *I want you* bit. Thing is, I want you too. So, what are we going to do about it?'

His gaze drifted to her mouth and then back to her eyes, his eyes hardening as if he had called on some inner strength to keep his self-control in check. 'We're going to ignore it, that's what.' His tone had the same determined edge as his gaze.

Sabrina moistened her lips, watching as his

gaze followed the movement of her tongue. 'What if I don't want to ignore it? What if I want you to kiss me? What if I want you to make love to me just this once? No one needs to know about it. It's just between us. It will get it out of our system once and for all and then we can go back to normal.'

She could hardly believe she had been so upfront. She had never been so brazen, so bold about her needs. But she could no longer ignore the pulsing ache of her body. The need that clawed and clenched. The need that only *he* triggered. Was that why she hadn't made love with anyone for all these years? No one made her feel this level of desire. No one even came close to stirring her flesh into a heated rush of longing.

'Sabrina…please…' His voice had a scraped-raw quality as if his throat had been scoured with a bristled brush.

'Please what? Don't tell it like it is?' Sabrina placed her hand on his chest where his heart was thud, thud, thudding so similar to her own. 'You want me. You said so. I felt it when you kissed me three weeks ago. And I know you want me now.'

Max took her by the hands, his fingers almost overlapping around her wrists. At first, she thought he was going to put her from him, but then his fingers tightened and he drew her closer. 'This is madness…' His smoky grey-blue gaze became hooded as it focussed on her mouth as if drawn to it by a magnetic force too powerful for his willpower.

'What is mad about two consenting adults having a one-night stand?' There she went again—such brazen words spilling out of her mouth, as if she'd swallowed the bad girl's guide to hook-up sex. Who was this person she had suddenly become since entering his hotel room? It wasn't anyone Sabrina recognised. But she wasn't going to stop now. She couldn't. If she didn't have sex with Max, someone she knew and trusted to take care of her, who else would she get to do the deed? No one, that's who.

Ten years had already passed and her confidence around men had gone backwards, not forwards. It was do or die—of sexual frustration. She wanted Max to cure her of her of her hangups…not that she was going to tell him about her lack of a love life. No flipping way. He'd get all knight-in-shining-armour about it and refuse to make love to her.

Max brushed the pad of his thumb over her bottom lip, pressing and then releasing until her senses were singing like the Philharmonic choir. 'A one-night stand? Is that really what you want?'

Sabrina fisted her hands into the thickness of his dark brown hair, the colour so similar to her own. She fixed her gaze on his troubled one. 'Make love to me, Max. Please?' *Gah*. Was she begging now? Was that how desperate she had become?

Yep. That desperate.

Max tipped up her chin, his eyes locking on hers. 'One night? No repeats? No happy ever after, right?'

Sabrina licked her lips—a mixture of nerves and feverish excitement. 'I want no one and I mean no one to find out about this. It will be our little secret. Agreed?'

One of his dark brows lifted above his sceptical gaze. But then his gaze flicked back to her mouth and he gave a shuddery sigh, as if the final restraint on his self-control had popped its bolts. 'Madness,' he said, so low she almost couldn't hear it. 'This is madness.' And then his mouth came down and set fire to hers.

CHAPTER FOUR

Six weeks later...

'SO, ARE YOU still keeping mum about what happened between you and Max in Venice?' Holly asked when she came into Sabrina's studio for a wedding-dress fitting.

Sabrina made a zipping-the-lips motion. 'Yep. I promised.'

Holly's eyes were twinkling so much they rivalled the sparkly bridal tiaras in the display cabinet. 'You can't fool me. I know you slept with him. What I don't understand is why you haven't continued sleeping with him. Was he that bad a lover?'

Sabrina pressed her lips together to stop herself from spilling all. So many times over the last six weeks she'd longed to tell Holly about that amazing night. About Max's amazing lovemaking. How he had made her feel. Her body hadn't felt the same since. She couldn't even think of him without having a fluttery sensation in her stomach. She had relived every touch of his hands and lips and tongue. She had repeatedly, obsessively dreamed about his possession, the way his body had moved within hers with such intense passion and purpose.

She picked up the bolt of French lace her friend had chosen and unrolled it over the cutting table. 'I'm not going to kiss and tell. It's…demeaning.'

'You kiss and told when he kissed you after he drove you home that night a few weeks back. Why not now?'

'Because I made a promise.'

'What?' Holly's smiling expression was exchanged for a frown. 'You don't trust me to keep it a secret? I'm your best friend. I wouldn't tell a soul.'

Sabrina glanced across the table at her friend. 'What about Zack? You guys share everything, right?'

Holly gnawed at her lip. 'Yeah, well, that's what people in love do.'

She tried to ignore the little dart of jealousy she felt at Holly's happiness. Her friend was preparing for her wedding to Zack Knight in a matter of weeks and what did Sabrina have on her love radar? Nothing. *Nada.* Zilch.

A mild wave of nausea assailed her. Was it possible to be lovesick without actually being in love? Okay. She was in love. In love with Max's lovemaking. Deeply in love. She couldn't stop thinking about him and the things he had done to her. The things they had done together. The things she had done to him. She placed a hand on her squeamish tummy and swallowed. She had to get a grip. She couldn't be bitter and sick to her stomach about her best friend's joy at marrying the man she loved. So what if Holly was having the most amazing sex with Zack while all Sabrina had was memories of one night with Max?

Holly leaned across the worktable. 'Hey, are you okay? You've gone as white as that French lace.'

Sabrina grimaced as her stomach contents swished and swirled and soured. 'I'm just feeling a little…off.'

Holly did a double blink. 'Off? As in nauseous?'

She opened her mouth to answer but had to clamp her hand over it because a surge of sickness rose up from her stomach. 'Excuse me…' Her hand muffled her choked apology and she bolted to the bathroom, not even stopping to close the door.

Holly came in behind her and handed her some paper towels from the dispenser on the wall. 'Is that a dodgy curry or too much champagne?'

Sabrina looked up from the toilet bowl. 'Ack. Don't mention food.'

Holly bent down beside her and placed a hand on Sabrina's shoulder. 'How long have you been feeling unwell?'

'Just today...' Sabrina swallowed against another tide of excessive saliva. 'I must have a stomach bug...or something...'

'Would the "or something" have anything to do with your weekend in Venice with Max, which you, obstinately and totally out of character, refuse to discuss?'

Sabrina's scalp prickled like army ants on a military parade. Max had used a condom. He'd used three over the course of the night. She was taking the lowest dose of the Pill to regulate her cycle because the others she'd tried had messed with her mood. 'I can't possibly be pregnant...'

Holly helped her to her feet. 'Are you saying you didn't sleep with him?'

Sabrina pulled her hair back from her face and sighed. 'Okay, so I did sleep with him. But you have to promise you won't tell anyone. Not even Zack.'

'Honey, I can trust Zack to keep it quiet.' Holly stroked Sabrina's arm. 'Did Max use a condom?'

Sabrina nodded. 'Three.'

Holly's eyes bulged. 'At a time?'

'No, we made love three times.' She closed the toilet seat and pressed the flush button. 'We made a promise not to talk about it. To anyone. Ever.'

'But why?'

Sabrina turned to wash her hands and face at the basin. 'We both agreed it was the best thing considering how our families go on and on about us getting together. We had a one-night stand to get it out of our system. End of story. Neither of us wants be involved with the other.'

'Or so *you* say.' Holly's tone was so sceptical she could have moonlighted as a detective.

Sabrina made a business of drying her face and hands. 'It's true. We would be hopeless as a couple. We fight all the time.'

Holly leaned against the door jamb, arms folded. 'Clearly not all the time if you had sex three times. Unless it was combative sex?'

Sabrina glanced at her friend in the reflection of the mirror. 'No…it wasn't combative sex. It was…amazing sex.' She had to stop speaking as the tiny frisson of remembered delight trickled over her flesh.

'Have you seen Max since that weekend?'

'No. We agreed to keep our distance as if nothing happened.' Sabrina sighed. 'He even checked out early from the hotel after our night together. He wasn't there when I woke up. He sent me a text from the airport to say he'd covered the bill for the suite and that's the last time I heard from him.' It had hurt to find the suite empty the next morning. Hurt badly. So much for her following the Fling Handbook guidelines. She'd foolishly expected a good morning kiss or two…or more.

'If you're not suffering from a stomach bug, then you'll have to see him sooner or later,' Holly said.

Sabrina put her hand on her abdomen, her heart beginning to pound with an echo of dread. She couldn't possibly be pregnant... *Could she?* What on earth would she say to Max? Max, who had already made it known he didn't want children. How could she announce *he* was the father of her child?

But wait, women had pregnancy scares all the time. Her cycle was crazy in any case. She had always planned to have kids, but not yet. She was still building up her business. Still trying to prove to her family her career choice was as viable, rewarding and fulfilling as theirs.

She'd had it all planned: get her business well established, hopefully one day fall in love with a man who would treat her the way she had always longed to be treated. Not that she had actively gone looking for the love of her life. She had been too worried about a repeat of her embarrassing falling-in-love episode during her teens. But getting married and having babies was what she wanted. One day. How could she have got it so messed up by falling pregnant? Now? While being on the Pill and using condoms? She was still living in a poky little bedsit, for God's sake.

Sabrina moved past Holly to get out of the bathroom. 'I can't tell him until I know for sure. I need to get a test kit. I have to do it today because there's a Midhurst and Firbank family gathering tomorrow night and I can't do a no-show. It's Max's mother's birthday. She'd be hurt if I didn't go.'

'You could say you've got a stomach bug.'

Sabrina gave her a side-eye. 'My parents and brothers will be there and once they hear I've got a stomach bug, one or all of them will be on my doorstep with their doctor's bag.' She clutched two handfuls of her hair with her hands. 'Argh. Why am I such a disaster? This wasn't meant to happen. Not *no-o-o-w.*' To her shame, her last word came as a childish wail.

'Oh, sweetie, you're not a disaster. Falling pregnant to a guy you love is not a catastrophe. Not in this day and age in any case.'

Sabrina dropped her hands from her head and glared at her friend. 'Who said I was in love with Max? Why do you keep going on about it?'

Holly placed her hands on her hips in an *I know you better than you do yourself* pose. 'Hello? You haven't slept with anyone for ten years, and then you spend a night in bed with a man you've known since you were in nappies? You wouldn't have slept with him if you didn't feel something for him.'

Sabrina rolled her lips together and turned away to smooth the fabric out on the worktable. 'Okay, so maybe I don't hate him as much as I used to, but I'm not in love with him. I wouldn't be so…so… stupid.' *Would she?* She had promised herself she would never find herself in that situation again. Fancying herself in love with someone who might reject her in the end like her teenage boyfriend had. Falling in love with Max would be asking for the sort of trouble she could do without. More trouble, that was, because finding herself pregnant to him was surely trouble enough.

Holly touched Sabrina on the arm. 'Do you want me to stay with you while you do the test?'

Sabrina gulped back a sob. 'Oh…would you?'

Holly smiled. 'That's what best friends are for—through thick and thin, and sick and sin, right?'

If it hadn't been his mother's birthday Max would have found some excuse to not show up. Not that he didn't want to see Sabrina. He did, which was The Problem. Wanting to see her, wanting to touch her, wanting to kiss her, wanting, wanting, wanting to make love to her again. He had told himself one night and one night only and here he was six weeks later still replaying every minute of that stolen night of seriously hot sex. Sex so amazing he could still feel aftershocks when he so much as pictured her lying in his arms. Sex so planet-dislodging he hadn't bothered hooking up with anyone else and wondered in his darkest moments if he ever would.

He couldn't imagine touching another woman after making love with Sabrina. How could he kiss another mouth as sweet and responsive as hers? How could he slide his hands down a body so lush and ripe and feminine if it didn't belong to Sabrina?

Max arrived at his parents' gracious home in Hampton Court, and after greeting his mother and father took up his usual place at the back of the crowded room to do his people-watching thing. He searched the sea of faces to see if Sabrina was among them, more than a little shocked at how disappointed he was not to find her. But then a thought shot like a stray dart into his brain. What if she brought someone with her? Another man? A new date? A man she was now sleeping with and doing all the sexy red-hot things she had done with him?

Max took a tumbler of spirits off the tray of a passing waiter and downed it in one swallow. He had to get a hold of himself. He was thirty-four years old, not some hormone-driven teenager suffering his first crush. So what if Sabrina slept with someone else? What business was it of his? They'd made an agreement of one night to get the lust bug out of the way.

No repeats.

No replays.

No sequel.

No happy-ever-after.

Max turned to put his empty glass down on a table next to him and saw Sabrina greeting his mother on the other side of the room. The way his parents adored her was understandable given they hadn't had any children after the loss of Daniel. Sabrina, as their only godchild, had been lavished with love and attention. Max knew their affection for her had helped them to heal as much as was possible after the tragic loss of an infant. Not that his parents hadn't adored him too. They had been fabulous parents trying to do their best after such sad circumstances, which, in an ill-advised but no less understandable way, had fed their little fantasy of him and Sabrina one day getting together and playing happy families.

But it was a step too far.

Way, way too far.

Sabrina finally stepped out of his mother's bone-crushing hug and met his gaze. Her eyes widened and then flicked away, her cheeks going an intense shade of pink. She turned and hurriedly made her way through the knot of guests and disappeared through the door that led out to the gallery-wide corridor.

Max followed her, weaving his way through the crowd just in time to see Sabrina scuttling into the library further down the corridor, like a terrified mouse trying to escape a notoriously cruel cat. In spite of the background noise of the party, the sound of the key turning in the lock was like a rifle shot. Or a slap on the face.

Okay, so he had left her in Venice without saying goodbye in person but surely that didn't warrant *this* type of reaction?

Max knocked on the library door. 'Sabrina? Let me in.'

He could hear the sound of her breathing on the other side of the door—hectic and panicked as if she really was trying to avoid someone menacing. But after a moment the key turned in the lock and the door creaked open.

'Are you alone?' Sabrina's voice sounded as creaky as the door, her eyes wide and bluer than he had ever seen them. And, he realised with a jolt, reddened as if she'd been recently crying. A lot.

'Yes, but what's going on?' He stepped into the room before she could stop him and closed the door behind him.

Sabrina took a few steps back and hugged her arms around her middle, her eyes skittering away from his. 'I have something to tell you…'

Here we go. Max had been here so many times before. The *I want more than a one-night stand* speech. But this time he was okay with it. More than okay. He could think of nothing he wanted more than to have a longer fling with her. Longer than one night, that was. A week or two, a month or three. Long enough to scratch the itch but not long enough for her to get silly ideas about it being for ever. 'It's okay, Sabrina. You don't have to look so scared. I've been thinking along the same lines.'

Her smooth brow crinkled into a frown. 'The same...lines?'

Max gave a soft laugh, his blood already pumping at the thought of taking her in his arms. Maybe even here in the quiet of the library while the guests were partying in the ballroom. What could be sexier than a clandestine affair? 'We'd have to keep it a secret, of course. But a month or two would be fun.' He took a step towards her but she backed away as if he was carrying the Black Plague.

'No.' She held up her hands like stop signs, her expression couldn't have looked more horrified than if he'd drawn a gun.

No? Max hadn't heard that word from a woman for a long time. Weird, but hearing it from Sabrina was unusually disappointing. 'Okay. That's fine. We'll stick to the original agreement.'

She gave an audible swallow and her arms went back around her middle. 'Max...' She slowly lifted her gaze back to his, hers still wide as Christmas baubles. 'I don't know how to tell you this...'

His gut suddenly seized and he tried to control his breathing. So she'd found someone else. No wonder his offer of a temporary fling had been turned down. She was sleeping with someone else. Someone else was kissing that beautiful mouth, someone else was holding her gorgeous body in their arms.

'It's okay, Sabrina.' How had he got his voice to sound so level? So damn normal when his insides were churning with jealousy? Yes, jealousy—that thing he never felt. Ever. Not for anyone. The big green-eyed monster was having a pity party in his gut and there was nothing he could do about it.

One of Sabrina's hands crept to press against her stomach. She licked her lips and opened her mouth to speak but couldn't seem to get her voice to work.

Max called on every bit of willpower he possessed to stop himself from reaching for her and showing her why a temporary fling with him was much a better idea than her getting involved permanently with someone else. A hard sell to a fairytale girl, but still. His hands stayed resolutely by his sides, but his fingers were clenching and unclenching like his jaw. 'Who is it?' There. He'd asked the question his pride had forbidden him to ask.

Sabrina's brow creased into another puzzled frown. 'I… You think there's someone…*else*?'

Max shrugged as if it meant nothing to him what she did and whom she did it with. But on the inside he was slamming his fist into the wall in frustration. Bam. Bam. Bam. The imaginary punches were in time with the thud, thud, thud of his heart. 'That's what this is about, isn't it?'

'Have *you* found someone else?' Her voice was faint and hesitant as if it was struggling to get past a stricture in her throat.

'Not yet.'

She closed her eyes in a tight squint as if his answer had pained her. She opened her eyes again and took a deep breath. 'In a way, this is about someone else…' She laced her fingers together in front of her stomach, then released them and did it again like a nervous tic. 'Someone neither of us has met…yet…'

Max wanted to wring his own hands. He wanted to turn back time and go back to Venice and do things differently. He had to get control of himself. He couldn't allow his jealousy over a man who may or may not exist to mess with his head. He took a calming breath, released it slowly. They would both eventually find someone else. He would have to get used to seeing her with a husband one day. A man who would give her the family she wanted. The commitment and the love she wanted. And Max would move from woman to woman just as he had been doing for the last six years. 'So, you're saying you're not actually seeing someone else right at this moment?'

'No.' Her face screwed up in distaste. 'How could you think I would want to after what we shared?'

'It was just sex, Sabrina.' He kept his tone neutral even though his male ego was doing fist pumps. Damn good sex. Amazing sex. Awesome sex he wanted to repeat. Then a victory chant sounded in his head. *There isn't anyone else. There isn't anyone else.* The big green monster slunk away and relief flooded Max's system.

'Yeah, well, if only it had been just sex…' Something about her tone and her posture made the hairs of the back of his neck stand up. Her hand kept creeping over the flat plane of her belly, her throat rising and falling over a swallow that sounded more like a gulp.

Max was finding it hard to make sense of what she was saying. And why was she looking so flustered? 'I'm not sure where this conversation is heading, but how about you say what you want to say, okay? I promise I won't interrupt. Just spit it out, for God's sake.'

Her eyes came back to his and she straightened her spine as if girding herself for a firing squad. 'Max… I'm pregnant.'

CHAPTER FIVE

MAX STEPPED BACK as if she had stabbed him. His gut even clenched as if a dagger had gone through to his backbone. *Pregnant?* The word was like a poison spreading through his blood, leaving a trail of catastrophic destruction in its wake. His heart stopped and started in a sickening boom-skip-boom-skip-boom-skip rhythm, his lungs almost collapsing as he fought to take a breath. His skin went hot, then cold, and his scalp prickled and tightened as if every hair was shrinking away in dread.

'You're…pregnant?' His voice cracked like an egg thrown on concrete, his mind splintering into a thousand panicked thoughts. A baby. They had made a baby. Somehow, in spite of all the protection he had used, they had made a baby. 'Are you sure?'

She pressed her lips together and nodded, her chin wobbling. 'I've done a test. Actually, I've done five. They were all positive.'

Max scraped a hand through his hair so roughly he nearly scalped himself. 'Oh, God…' He turned away, a part of him vainly hoping that when he turned back he wouldn't find himself in the library of his parents' mansion with Sabrina telling him he was to be a father. It was like a bad dream. A nightmare.

His. Personal. Nightmare.

'Thanks for not asking if it's yours.' Sabrina's soft voice broke through his tortured reverie.

He swung back to face her; suddenly conscious of how appallingly he was taking her announcement. But nothing could have prepared him for this moment. He had never in his wildest imaginings ever thought he would be standing in front of a woman—any woman—bearing this bombshell news. Pregnant. A baby. *His* baby. 'I'm sorry, but it's such a shock.' Understatement. His heart was pounding so hard he wouldn't have been out of place on a critical care cardiac ward. Sweat was pouring down between his shoulder blades. Something was scrabbling and scratching like there was a frantic animal trapped in his guts.

He stepped towards her and held out his hands but she stepped back again. His hands fell back by his sides. 'So…what have you decided to do?'

Her small neat chin came up and her cornflower-blue eyes hardened with determination. 'I'm not having a termination. Please don't ask me to.'

Max flinched. 'Do you really think I'm the sort of man to do something like that? I'm firmly of the opinion that it's solely a woman's choice whether she continues with a pregnancy or not.'

Relief washed over her pinched features but there was still a cloud of worry in her gaze. 'I'm not against someone else making that difficult choice but I can't bring myself to do it. Not under these circumstances. I don't expect you to be involved if that's not what you want. I know this is a terrible shock and not something you want, but I thought you should know about the pregnancy first, before it becomes obvious, I mean.' Her hand went protectively to her belly again. 'I won't even tell people it's yours if you'd rather not have them know.'

Max was ashamed that for a nanosecond he considered that as an option. But how could he call himself a man and ignore his own flesh and blood? It wasn't the child's fault so why should it be robbed of a relationship with its father? He had grown up with a loving and involved father and couldn't imagine how different his life might have been without the solid and dependable support of his dad.

No. He would do the right thing by Sabrina and the baby. He would try his hardest not to fail them like he had failed his baby brother and his parents. He stepped forward and captured her hands before she could escape. 'I want my child to have my name. We'll marry as soon as I can arrange it.'

Sabrina pulled out of his hold as if his hands had burned her. 'You don't have to be so old-fashioned about it, Max. I'm not asking you to marry me.'

'I'm not asking you. I'm telling you what's going to happen.' As proposals went, Max knew it wasn't flash. But he'd proposed in a past life and he had sworn he would never do it again. But this was different. This was about duty and responsibility, not foolish, fleeting, fickle feelings. 'We will marry next month.'

'Next month?' Her eyes went round in shock. 'Are you crazy? This is the twenty-first century. Couples don't have to marry because they happened to get pregnant. No one is holding a gun to your head.'

'Do you really think I would walk away from the responsibility to my own flesh and blood? We will marry and that's final.'

Sabrina's eyes flashed blue sparks of defiance and her hands clenched into fists. 'You could do with some work on your proposal, buddy. No way am I marrying you. You don't love me.'

'So? You don't love me either,' Max said. 'This is not about us. This is about the baby we've made.

You need someone to support you and that someone is me. I won't take no for an answer.'

Her chin came up so high she could have given
a herd of mules a master class in stubbornness.
'Then we're at an impasse because no way am
I marrying a man who didn't even have the de-
cency to say goodbye in person the night we…
had sex.'

Max blew out a breath and shoved a hand back
through his hair again. 'Okay, so my exit might
have lacked a little finesse, but I didn't want you
to get any crazy ideas about our one night turning
into something else.'

'Oh, yeah? Well, because of the quality of your
stupid condoms, our one-night has turned into
something else—a damn baby!' She buried her
face in her hands and promptly burst into tears.

Max winced and stepped towards her, gathering her close against his body. This time she didn't
resist, and he wrapped his arms around her as the
sobs racked her slim frame. He stroked the back
of her silky head, his mind whirling with emotions he had no idea how to handle. Regret, shame
and blistering anger at himself. He had done this
to her. He had got her pregnant. Had the condoms
failed? He was always so careful. He always wore
one. No exceptions. Had he left it on too long? At
one point he had fallen asleep with her wrapped

in his arms, his body still encased in the warm wet velvet of hers.

Was that when it had happened? He should never have given in to the temptation of touching her. He had acted on primal instinct, ruled by his hormones instead of his head. 'I'm sorry. So sorry. But I thought you said you were on the Pill?'

She eased away from his chest to look up at him through tear-washed eyes. 'I'm on a low dose one but I was so caught up with nerves about the expo, I had an upset tummy the day before I left for Venice. Plus, I was sick after having that champagne at the cocktail party.' She tried to suppress a hiccup but didn't quite manage it.

Max brushed the hair back from her face. 'Look, no one is to blame for this other than me. I shouldn't have touched you. I shouldn't have kissed you that first time and I definitely shouldn't have booked you into my room and—'

'Do you really regret what happened between us that night?' Her expression reminded him of a wounded puppy—big eyes, long face, fragile hope.

He cradled her face in his hands. 'That's the whole trouble. I don't regret it. Not a minute of it. I've thought of that night thousands of times since then.' He brushed his thumbs over her cheeks while still cupping her face. 'We'll make this work, Sabrina. We might not love each other in the traditional way, but we can make do.'

She tugged his hands away from her face and stepped a metre away to stand in front of the floor-to-ceiling bookshelves. 'Make do? Is that all you want out of life? To…' she waved her hand in a sweeping gesture '…*make do*? What about love? Isn't that an essential ingredient of a good marriage?'

'I'm not offering you that sort of marriage.'

Her eyes flashed and she planted her hands on her hips. 'Well, guess what? I'm not accepting *that* sort of proposal.'

'Would you prefer me to lie to you?' Max tried to keep his voice steady but he could feel ridges of anger lining his throat. 'To get down on bended knee and say a whole lot of flowery words we both know I don't mean?'

'Did you say them to Lydia?'

'Let's keep Lydia out of this.' This time the anger nearly choked him. He hated thinking about his proposal six years ago to his ex-fiancée. He hated thinking about his failure to see the relationship for what it had been—a mistake from start to finish. It had occurred to him only recently that he had asked Lydia to marry him so his parents would back off about Sabrina. Not the best reason, by anyone's measure.

'You still have feelings for her, don't you? That's why you can't commit to anyone else.'

Max rolled his eyes and gave a short bark of a

laugh. 'Oh, please spare me the pop psychoanalysis. No, I do not still love Lydia. In fact, I never loved her.'

Sabrina blinked rapidly. 'Then why did you ask her to marry you?'

He walked over to the leather-topped mahogany desk and picked up the paperweight he had given his father when he was ten. He passed it from hand to hand, wondering how to answer. 'Good question,' he said, putting the paperweight down and turning to look at her. 'When we first dated, she seemed fine with my decision not to have kids. We had stuff in common, books, movies, that sort of thing.' He gave a quick open-close movement of his lips. 'But clearly it wasn't enough for her.'

'It might not have been about the kid thing. It might have been because she knew you didn't love her. I never thought your chemistry with her was all that good.'

Max moved closer to her, drawn by a force he couldn't resist. 'Unlike ours, you mean?' He traced a line from below her ear to her chin with his finger, watching as her pupils darkened and her breath hitched. Her spring flowers perfume danced around his nostrils, her warm womanly body making his blood thrum and hum and drum with lust. *Don't touch her.* His conscience pinged with a reminder but he ignored it.

Her hands came up to rest against his chest, the tip of her tongue sweeping over her rosebud lips. But then her eyes hardened and she pushed back from him and put some distance between them. 'I know what you're trying to do but it won't work. I will not be seduced into marrying you.'

'For God's sake, Sabrina,' Max said. 'This is not about seducing you into changing your mind. You're having my baby. I would never leave you to fend for yourself. That's not the sort of man I am.'

'Look, I know you mean well, but I can't marry you. I'm only just pregnant. I can't bear the thought of everyone talking about me, judging me for falling pregnant after a one-night stand, especially to you when I've done nothing but criticise you for years. Anyway, what if I were to have a miscarriage or something before the twelve-week mark? Then you'd hate me for sure for trapping you in a marriage neither of us wanted in the first place.'

The mention of miscarriage gave him pause. He had seen his mother go through several of them before and after the death of Daniel. It had been torture to watch her suffer not just physically but emotionally. The endless tears, the longing looks at passing prams or pregnant women. He had been young, but not too young to notice the despair on his mother's face. 'Okay. So we will wait until the twelve-week mark. But I'm only compromising because it makes sense to keep this news to ourselves until then.'

Sabrina bit her lower lip and it made him want to kiss away the indentation her teeth made when she released it. 'I've kind of told Holly. She was with me when I did the test.'

'Can you trust her to keep it to herself?'

'She'll probably tell Zack, but she assures me he won't blab either.'

Max stepped closer again and took her hands, stroking the backs of them with his thumbs. 'How are you feeling? I'm sorry I didn't ask earlier. Not just about how you're feeling about being pregnant but are you sick? Is there anything you need?'

Fresh tears pooled in her eyes and she swallowed a couple of times. 'I'm a bit sick and my breasts are a little tender.'

'Is it too early to have a scan?'

'I'm not sure, I haven't been to see the doctor yet.'

'I'll go with you to all of your appointments, that is, if you want me there?' Who knew he could be such a model father-to-be? But, then, he figured he'd had a great role model in his own dad. Even so, he wanted to be involved for the child's sake.

'Do you want to be there or would you only be doing it out of duty?'

'I want to be there to see our baby for the first time.' Max was a little surprised to realise how much he meant it. But he needed to see the baby to believe this pregnancy had really happened. He still felt as if he'd stepped into a parallel universe. Could his and Sabrina's DNAs really be getting it on inside her womb? A baby. A little person who would look like one or the other, or a combination of both of them. A child who would grow up and look to him for protection and nurturing. Did he trust himself to do a good job? How could he when he had let his baby brother down so badly?

The door suddenly opened behind them and Max glanced over his shoulder to see his mother standing there. 'Oh, there you two are.' Her warm brown eyes sparkled with fairy godmother delight.

Sabrina sprang away from Max but she bumped into the mahogany desk behind her and yelped. 'Ouch!'

Max reached for Sabrina, steadying her by bringing her close to his side. 'Are you okay?'

She rubbed her left hip, her cheeks a vivid shade of pink. 'Yes…'

'Did I startle you?' Max's mother asked. 'Sorry, darling, but I was wondering where you'd gone. You seemed a little upset earlier.'

'I'm not upset,' Sabrina said, biting her lip.

His mother raised her eyebrows and then glanced at Max. 'I hope you two aren't fighting again? No wonder the poor girl gets upset with you glaring at her all the time. I don't want my party spoilt by your boorish behaviour. Why can't you just kiss and make up for a change?'

Max could have laughed at the irony of the situation if his sense of humour hadn't already been on life support. He'd done way more than kiss Sabrina and now there were consequences he would be dealing with for the rest of his life. But there was no way he could tell his mother what had gone on between them. No way he could say anything until she was through the first trimester of her pregnancy. It would get everybody's hopes up and the pressure would be unbearable—even more unbearable than it already was.

'It's fine, Aunty Gillian. Max is being perfectly civil to me,' Sabrina said, carefully avoiding his gaze.

Max's mother shifted her lips from side to side. 'Mmm, I'm not sure it's safe to leave you two alone for more than five minutes. Who knows what might happen?'

Who knew, indeed?

As soon as the door closed behind Gillian Firbank, Sabrina swung her gaze to Max. 'Do you think she suspects anything?'

'I don't think so. But we have to keep our relationship quiet until you get through the first trimester. Then we can tell everyone we're marrying.'

She stared at him, still not sure how to handle this change in him. So much for the one night and one night only stance he'd taken before. Now he was insisting on marrying her and wouldn't take no for an answer.

She blew out a breath, whirled away and crossed her arms over her middle. 'You're being ridiculous, Max. We can't do this. We can't get married just because I'm pregnant. We'd end up hating each other even more than we do now.'

'When have I ever said I hated you?' Max's jaw looked like it was set in stone. A muscle moved in and out next to his flattened mouth as if he was mentally counting to ten. And his smoky blue eyes smouldered, making something fizz at the back of her knees like sherbet.

'You don't have to say it. It's in your actions. You can barely speak to me without criticising something about me.'

He came to her and before she could move away he took her by the upper arms in a gentle but firm hold. Deep down, Sabrina knew she'd had plenty of time to escape those warm strong fingers, but right then her body was craving his touch. Six long weeks had passed since their stolen night of passion and now she was alone with him, her senses were firing, her needs clamouring, her resolve to resist him faltering. 'I don't hate you, Sabrina.'

But you don't love me either.

She didn't say the words out loud but the silence seemed to ring with their echo. 'We'd better get back to the party otherwise people will start talking.'

His hands tightened. 'Not yet.' His voice was low and deep and husky, his eyes flicking to her mouth as if drawn by a force he couldn't counteract.

Sabrina breathed in the clean male scent of him, the hint of musk, the base note of bergamot and a top note of lemon. She leaned towards him, pushed by the need to feel him close against her, to feel his body respond to hers. He stirred against her, the tempting hardness of his body reminding hers of everything that had passed between them six weeks ago. 'Max… I can't think straight when you touch me.'

'Then don't think.'

She stepped out of his hold with a willpower she hadn't known she possessed. 'I need a couple of weeks to get my head around this…situation. It's been such a shock and I don't want to rush into anything I might later regret.'

She didn't want to think about all the madly-in-love brides who came to her for their wedding dresses. She didn't want to think about Max's offer, which had come out of a sense of duty instead of love. But she didn't want to think about bringing up a baby on her own either. She walked to the library door, knowing that if she stayed a minute longer she would end up in his arms.

'Where are you going?' Max asked.

She glanced over her shoulder. 'The party, remember?'

He dragged a hand over his face and scowled. 'I hate parties.'

CHAPTER SIX

BY THE TIME Max dragged himself out of the library to re-join the party there was no sign of Sabrina. He moved through the house, pretending an interest in the other guests he was nowhere near feeling, surreptitiously sweeping his gaze through the crowd to catch a glimpse of her. He didn't want to make it too obvious he was looking for her, but he didn't want her to leave his parents' house until he was sure she was okay.

He was having enough trouble dealing with the shock news of her pregnancy, so he could only imagine how it was impacting on her. Even though he knew she had always wanted children, she wanted them at the right time with the right guy. He wasn't that guy. But it was too late to turn back the clock. He was the father of her child and there was no way he was going to abandon her, even if he had to drag her kicking, screaming and swearing to the altar.

Max wandered out into the garden where large

scented candles were burning in stands next to the formal garden beds. There was no silky honey-brown head in the crowd gathered outside. The sting of disappointment soured his mood even further. The only way to survive one of his parents' parties was to spar with Sabrina. He hadn't realised until then how much he looked forward to it. Was he weird or what? Looking forward to their unfriendly fire was not healthy. It was sick.

And so too was wanting to make love to a woman you got pregnant six weeks ago. But he couldn't deny the longing that was pounding through him. He'd wanted to kiss her so badly back in the library. Kiss her and hold her and remind her of the chemistry they shared. Hadn't it always been there? The tension that vibrated between them whenever their gazes locked. How the slightest touch of her hand sent a rocket charge through his flesh. That first kiss all those weeks ago had set in motion a ferocious longing that refused to be suppressed.

But it *had* to be suppressed. It *must* be suppressed. He was no expert on pregnancy, having avoided the topic for most of his adult life, but wasn't sex between the parents dangerous to the baby under some circumstances? Particularly if the pregnancy was a high-risk one? How could he live with himself if he harmed the baby before it even got a chance to be born? Besides, he didn't want their families to get too excited about him and Sabrina seeing each other. He could only imagine his mother's disappointment if she thought she was going to be a grandmother only to have it snatched away from her if Sabrina's pregnancy failed.

No. He would do the noble thing. He would resist the temptation and get her safely through to the twelve-week mark. Even if it damn near killed him.

Max's mother came towards him with half a glass of champagne in her hand. 'Are you looking for Sabrina?'

'No.' *Shoot.* He'd delivered his flat denial far too quickly.

'Well, if you are, then you're wasting your time. She went home half an hour ago. Said she wasn't feeling well. I hope it wasn't your fault?' The accusatory note in his mother's voice grated along his already frayed nerves.

Yep, it was definitely his fault.

Big time.

Sabrina managed to make it back to her tiny flat without being sick. The nausea kept coming and going in waves and she'd been worried it might grip her in the middle of the party celebrations. She had decided it was safer to make her excuses and leave. Besides, it might have looked suspicious if her mother or Max's noticed she wasn't drinking the champagne. After all, the party girl with a glass of bubbles in her hand and a dazzling smile on her face whilst working the room was her signature style.

But it seemed Sabrina had left one party to come home to another. The loud music coming from the upstairs flat was making the walls shake. How would she ever get to sleep with that atrocious racket going on? She only hoped the party wouldn't go on past midnight. Last time the neighbours had held a party the police had been called because a scuffle had broken out on the street as some of the guests had been leaving.

It wasn't the nicest neighbourhood to live in— certainly nowhere as genteel as the suburbs where her parents and two older brothers lived and where she had spent her childhood. But until she felt more financially stable she didn't feel she had a choice. Rents in London were continually on the rise, and with the sharing economy going from strength to strength, it meant there was a reduced number of properties available for mid- to long-term rent.

She peeled off her clothes and slipped her nightgown over her head. She went to the bathroom and took off her makeup but then wished she hadn't. Was it possible to look that pale whilst still having a functioning pulse?

Sabrina went back to her bedroom and climbed into bed and pulled the covers over her head, but the sound of heavy footsteps clattering up and down the stairs would have made a herd of elephants sound like fairies' feet. Then, to add insult to injury, someone began to pound on her front door.

'Argh.' She threw off the covers and grabbed her wrap to cover her satin nightgown and padded out to check who was there through the peephole. No way was she going to open the door if it was a drunken stranger. But a familiar tall figure stood there with a brooding expression. 'Max?'

'Let me in.' His voice contained the thread of steel she had come to always associate with him.

She unlocked the door and he was inside her flat almost before she could step out of the way. 'What are you doing here?'

He glanced around the front room of her flat like a construction official inspecting a condemned building. 'I'm not letting you stay here. There isn't even an intercom on this place. It's not safe.'

Pride stiffened her spine and she folded her arms across her middle. 'I don't plan to stay here for ever but it's all I can afford. Anyway, you didn't seem to think it was too unsafe when you kissed me that time you brought me home.'

'My mind was on other things that night.' There was the sound of a bottle breaking in the stairwell and he winced. 'Right. That settles it. Get dressed and pack a bag. You're coming with me.'

Sabrina unfolded her arms and placed them on

her hips. 'You can't just barge into my home and tell me what to do.'

'Watch me, sweetheart.' He moved past her and went to her bedroom, opening drawers and cupboards and throwing a collection of clothes on the bed.

Sabrina followed him into her bedroom. 'Hey, what the hell do you think you're doing?'

'If you won't pack, then I'll do it for you.' He opened another cupboard and found her overnight bag and, placing it on the bed, began stuffing her clothes into it.

Sabrina grabbed at the sweater he'd picked up and pulled on it like a dog playing tug-of-war. 'Give it back.' *Tug. Tug. Tug.* 'You're stretching it out of shape.'

He whipped it out of her hands and tossed it in the bag on the bed. 'I'll buy you a new one.' He slammed the lid of the bag down and zipped it up with a savage movement. 'I'm not letting you stay another minute in this hovel.'

'Hovel?' Sabrina snorted. 'Did you hear that clanging noise? Oh, yes, that must be the noise of all those silver spoons hanging out of your mouth.'

His grey-blue eyes were as dark as storm clouds with lightning flashes of anger. 'Why do you live like this when you could live with your parents until you get on your feet?'

'Hello? I'm twenty-eight years old,' Sabrina

said. 'I haven't lived with my parents for a decade. And nor would I want to. They'd bombard me constantly with all of your amazingly wonderful assets until I went stark certifiably crazy.'

There was the sound of someone shouting and swearing in the stairwell and Max's jaw turned to marble. 'I can't let you stay here, Sabrina. Surely you can understand that?'

She sent him a glare. 'I understand you want to take control.'

'This is not about control. This is about your safety.' He scraped a hand through his hair. 'And the baby's safety too.'

Sabrina was becoming too tired to argue. The noise from upstairs was getting worse and there would be no hope of sleeping even if by some remote chance she convinced Max to leave her be. Besides, she secretly hated living here. The landlord was a creep and kept threatening to put up the rent.

Sabrina was too proud, too determined to prove to her parents she didn't need their help. But it wasn't just herself she had to think about now. She had to take care of the baby. She'd read how important it was for mothers-to-be to keep stress levels down and get plenty of rest for the sake of the developing foetus. Was Max thinking along the same lines? 'Why did you come here tonight?' she asked.

'I was worried about you. You left the party early and I worried you might be sick or faint whilst driving home. I'm sorry. I should have offered to drive you but I was still reeling from your news and—'

'It's okay.' She tossed her hair back over one shoulder. 'As you see, I managed to get home in one piece.'

He stepped closer and took her hands in his. His touch made every nerve in her skin fizz, his concerned gaze striking a lethal blow to her stubborn pride. 'Let me look after you, Sabrina. Come home with me.'

Her insides quivered, her inner core recalling his intimate presence. The memories of that night seemed to be swirling in the air they shared. Her body was so aware of his proximity she could feel every fibre of her satin nightgown against her flesh. Was he remembering every moment of that night? Was his body undergoing the same little pulses and flickers of remembered pleasure? 'Live with you, you mean?'

'We'll have separate rooms.'

She frowned. 'You don't want to…?'

'I don't think it's a good idea.' He released her hands and stepped back. 'Not until you get through the first trimester. Then we'll reassess.' His tone was so matter-of-fact he could have been reading a financial report.

Sabrina couldn't quell her acute sense of disappointment. He didn't want her any more? Or maybe he did but he was denying himself because he'd set conditions on their relationship. 'But how will we keep our…erm…relationship or whatever we're now calling it a secret from our families if we're living under the same roof?'

'In some ways, it'll make it easier. We won't be seen out and about together in public. And I travel a lot for work so we won't be on top of each other.'

Doubts flitted through her mind like frenzied moths. Sharing a house with him was potentially dangerous. Her body was aflame with lust as soon as he came near, living with him would only make it a thousand times worse. She ached to feel his arms around her, his kiss on her mouth, his body buried within hers. What if she made a fool of herself? Wanting him so badly she begged him to make love to her?

What if she fell in love with him?

He wasn't offering her love, only his protection. Food and shelter and a roof over her head. And a stable but loveless marriage if the pregnancy continued. But wasn't that a pathway to heartbreak? How could she short-change herself by marrying someone who wasn't truly in love with her?

Max came closer again and took her hands. 'This is the best way forward. It will ensure your safety and my peace of mind.'

She looked down at their joined hands, his skin so tanned compared to the creamy whiteness of hers. It reminded her of the miracle occurring inside her body, the cells dividing, DNA being exchanged, traits and features from them both being switched on or off to make a whole new little person. A little person she was already starting to love. 'I don't know...'

His hands gave hers a small squeeze. 'Let's give it a try for the next few weeks, okay?'

Sabrina let out a sigh and gave him a wry glance. 'You know, you're kind of scaring me at how convincing you can be when you put your mind to it.'

He released her hands and stepped back with an unreadable expression. 'I'll wait for you out here while you get changed out of your nightgown. Any toiletries you need from the bathroom before we get going?'

She sighed and turned back for the bedroom. 'I'll get them once I've got changed.'

Max waited for Sabrina while she gathered her makeup and skincare products from the bathroom. He would have paced the floor but there wasn't the space for it. He would have taken out a window with his elbow each time he turned. It was true that he hadn't noticed how appalling her flat was when he'd brought her home that night all those weeks ago. The flat wasn't so bad inside—she had done her best to tart things up with brightly coloured scatter cushions and throw rugs over the cheap sofa, cute little knick-knacks positioned here and there and prints of artwork on the walls. There was even a bunch of fresh flowers, presumably supplied by her best friend Holly, who was a florist.

But it was what was on the outside of Sabrina's front door that worried him. Apart from the stale cooking smells, there were no security cameras, no intercom to screen the people coming in and out of the building. How could he sleep at night if he left her here with who knew what type of people milling past? Criminals? Drug dealers? Violent thugs?

No. It was safer for her at his house. Well, safe in one sense, dangerous in another. He had made a promise to himself that he would keep his hands off her. He knew he was locking the stable door even though the horse was well on its way to the maternity ward, but he had to be sensible about this. Sleeping with her before the three-month mark would make it even harder to end their relationship if the pregnancy failed.

Something tightened in his gut at the thought of her losing that baby. *His* baby. He had never imagined himself as a father. For most of his life he had blocked it out of his mind. He wasn't the type of man who was comfortable around kids. He actively avoided babies. One of his friends from university had asked him to be godfather to his firstborn son. Max had almost had a panic attack at the church when his friend's wife had handed him the baby to hold.

But now *he* was going to be a father.

Sabrina came out after a few minutes dressed in skinny jeans and a dove-grey boyfriend sweater that draped sensually over her bra-less breasts. On her feet she was wearing ballet slippers, and on her face an expression that was one part resignation and one part defiance. He tore his gaze away from the tempting globes of her breasts, remembering how soft they had felt in his hands, how tightly her nipples had peaked when he'd sucked on them. In a few months her body would be ripe with his child.

A child *he* had planted in her womb.

He had never considered pregnancy to be sexy but somehow with Sabrina it was. Damn it, everything about her was sexy. Wasn't that why he'd crossed the line and made love to her last month in Venice?

But now he had drawn a new line and there was no way he was stepping over it.

No. Freaking. Way.

Sabrina hadn't realised she had slept during the drive from her flat to Max's house in Notting Hill. She woke up when the car stopped and straightened from her slumped position in the passenger seat. She hadn't been to this new house of his before—but not for want of trying by his and her parents. She had walked past it once or twice but was always so keen to avoid him that she had stopped coming to the Portobello Road markets for fear of running into him.

The house was one in a long row of grand four-storey white terrace houses. Each one had a black wrought-iron balustrade on the second-floor balcony and the same glossy black decorative fencing at street level.

When Max led the way inside, she got a sense of what Lizzie Bennet in *Pride and Prejudice* had felt when seeing Pemberley, Mr Darcy's estate, for the first time. *This could be your home if you marry him.*

She turned in a circle in the black and white tiled foyer, marvelling at the décor that was stylish and elegant without being over the top. The walls and ceiling were a bone white but the chandelier overhead was a black one with sparkling crystal pendants that tinkled with the movement of air. There was a staircase leading to the upper floors, carpeted with a classic Persian runner with brass rods running along the back of each step to hold it in place. Works of art hung at various points, which she could only presume were originals. He didn't strike her as the sort of man to be content with a couple of cheap knock-offs to adorn his walls, like she had done at her flat.

'I'll show you to your room,' Max said. 'Or would you like something to eat and drink first?'

Sabrina tried to smother a yawn. 'No, I think I'll go straight to bed. I'm exhausted.'

He carried her small bag and led the way up the stairs, glancing back at her every few steps to make sure she was managing okay. It would have been touching if it hadn't been for how awkward the situation between them was. She was very much aware of how she had rocked his neat and ordered life with her bombshell news. She was still trying to come to terms with it herself. How was she going to run her business and look after a baby? What was she going to say to her parents and brothers?

Oh, by the way, I got myself knocked up by my mortal enemy Max Firbank.

'I'll show you around tomorrow, but the main bathroom is on the ground floor, along with the kitchen and living areas,' Max said. 'On this floor there's my study, second door on the left, and the guest bedrooms, each with its own bathroom. My room is on the third floor. There's a gym on the top floor.'

Sabrina stopped on the second-floor landing to catch her breath. 'Who needs a gym with all these stairs?'

He frowned and touched her on the arm. 'Are you okay?'

'Max, I'm fine. Please stop fussing.'

He drew in a breath and released it in a whoosh, his hand falling away from her forearm. 'Tomorrow I'll have the rest of your things brought over from your flat.'

'How am I going to explain why I'm not at home if my parents or brothers drop by? Where will I say I'm staying?'

'Tell them you're staying with a friend.'

Sabrina arched her eyebrows. 'Is that what you are now? My…friend?'

He glanced at her mouth before meeting her gaze with his inscrutable one. 'If we're going to be bringing up a child together then we'd damn well better not be enemies.'

She had a feeling he was fighting hard not to touch her. One of his hands was clenching and un-clenching and his chiselled jaw was set in a taut line. 'This is your worst nightmare, isn't it? Having me here, pregnant with a baby you didn't want.'

'Let's not talk any more tonight. We're both tired and—'

'I'm not so tired that I can't see how much you're hating this. Hating *me*.' She banged her fist against her chest for emphasis. 'I didn't do it deliberately, you know.'

'I never said you did.'

Sabrina was struggling to contain her over-wrought emotions. Her life was spiralling out of her control and there was nothing she could do about it. She swallowed a sob but another one followed it. She turned away and squeezed her eyes shut to stop the sting of tears.

Max put the bag down and placed his hands on her shoulders, gently turning her to face him, his expression etched with concern. 'Hey…' His finger lifted her face so her eyes met his. 'Listen to me, Sabrina. I do not hate you. Neither do I blame you for what's happened. I take full responsibility. And because of that, I want to take care of you in whatever way you need.'

But I need you. The words stayed silent on her tongue. She would not beg him to make love to her again. She wanted him to own his desire for her. To own it instead of denying it. She blinked the moisture away from her eyes. 'I'm worried about how I'll cope with my work and a baby. What if I lose my business? I've worked so hard to get it to this stage.'

His hands tightened on her shoulders. 'You will not lose your business. You can appoint a manager or outsource some work. The golden rule in running a business is only to do the stuff that only you can do.'

'I've been trying to do that by hiring a part-time assistant but she messed up my booking for Venice,' Sabrina said.

'It takes time to build up your confidence in your staff but if you train them to do things the way you want them done, and check in occasionally to see if they're on track, then things will eventually run the way you want them to.' He removed his hands from her shoulders and picked up her bag again. 'Now, young lady, it's time for you to get some shut-eye.'

He led her to one of the guest bedrooms further down the corridor. It was beautifully decorated in cream and white with touches of gold. The queen-sized bed was made up with snowy white bedlinen, the collection of standard and European pillows looking as soft as clouds. The cream carpet threatened to swallow her feet up to the ankle and she slipped off her shoes and sighed as her toes curled against the exquisite comfort of luxury fibres.

Max put Sabrina's bag on a knee-high chest near the built-in wardrobes. 'I'll leave you to settle in. The bathroom is through there. I'll see you in the morning.' His tone was so clipped he could have trimmed a hedge. He walked the door to leave and she wondered if he was thinking about the last time they had been alone together in a room with a bed. Did he regret their lovemaking so much that he couldn't bear the thought of repeating it? It felt uncomfortably like her boyfriend walking away, rejecting her. Hurting her.

'Max?'

He turned back to face her. 'Yes?'

Sabrina had to interlace her fingers in front of her body to keep from reaching out to him. She couldn't beg him to stay with her. Wouldn't beg him. The risk of him rejecting her would be too painful. 'Nothing…' A weak smile flickered across her lips. 'Goodnight.'

''Night.' And then he left and closed the door with a firm click.

CHAPTER SEVEN

MAX WENT DOWNSTAIRS before he was tempted to join Sabrina in that damn bed. What was wrong with him? Hadn't he done enough damage? He wanted slip in between those sheets with her, even if just to hold her against his body. He hadn't forgotten how it felt to have her satin-soft skin against his. He hadn't forgotten how it felt to glide his hands over her gorgeous breasts or how it felt to bury himself deep into her velvet warmth.

But he must *not* think about her like that. He had to keep his distance otherwise things could get even more complicated than they already were. Relationships got complicated when feelings were involved and he was already fighting more feelings than he wanted to admit. Everything was different about his relationship with Sabrina. Everything. And if that wasn't enough of a warning for him to back off in the feelings department, he didn't know what was.

He couldn't remember the last time he'd had a

sleepover with a lover. It hadn't been in this house as he'd only moved in a few months ago once the renovations had been completed. He hadn't even shared his previous house with Lydia in spite of her broad hints to move in with him.

Max sat at his desk in his study and sighed. For the next six weeks he would have to make sure he kept his relationship with Sabrina completely platonic. Since when had he found it sexy to make love to a pregnant woman? But now he couldn't stop thinking about the changes her body was undergoing.

Changes *he* had caused.

His gaze went to the framed photograph of his family on his desk. It had been taken just days before Daniel had died. His mother and father were sitting either side of him and he was holding his brother across his lap. Everyone was smiling, even Daniel.

Max wondered if he would ever be able to look at that photograph without regret and guilt gnawing at his insides. Regret and guilt and anger at himself for not doing more to help his little brother. It had taken many years for his parents to smile again, especially his mother.

Would the birth of his parents' first grandchild heal some of the pain of the past?

When Sabrina woke the next morning, it took her a moment to realise where she was. The room was bathed in golden sunlight, and she stretched like a lazy cat against the marshmallow-soft pillows. It was a Sunday so there was no rush to get out of bed…although staying in bed would be a whole lot more tempting if Max was lying here beside her. She'd heard him come up the stairs to his room on the floor above hers in the early hours of the morning. Didn't the man need more than three or four hours of sleep?

There was a tap at the door and she sat up in the bed. 'Come in.'

Max opened the door, deftly balancing a tray on one hand as he came in. 'Good morning. I thought you might like some tea and toast.'

'Oh, lovely, I haven't had breakfast in bed in ages.'

He came over to the bed and placed the tray, which had fold-down legs, across her lap. This close she could smell his freshly shampooed hair and the citrus fragrance of his aftershave. He straightened and gave his version of a smile. 'How are you feeling?'

'So far, so good,' Sabrina said. 'Sometimes the nausea hits when I first stand up.'

'Good reason to stay where you are, then.'

She picked up the steaming cup of tea and took a sip. 'Mmm…perfect. How did you know I take it black?'

His expression was wry. 'I think it's safe to say

your parents have told me just about everything there is to know about you over the years.'

Not quite everything.

Sabrina had never told her parents about her first sexual experience. The only person she'd told was Holly. It was too embarrassing, too painful to recall the shame she'd felt to hear such horrible rumours spread about her after giving herself to her boyfriend. 'Seriously, they told you how I take my tea?'

He gave a half smile. 'Only joking. No, I've been observing you myself.'

She put her tea back on the tray and picked up a slice of toast and peeped at him from half-lowered lashes. 'I've noticed.'

'Oh?'

'Yep. You got really annoyed when I danced with one of the guys at that party at my parents' house a few months back.' She nibbled on the toast and watched his expression go from that mercurial smile to a brooding frown. She pointed the toast at him. 'There. That's exactly how you looked that night.'

He rearranged his features back into a smile but it didn't involve his eyes. 'You imagined it. I was probably frowning about something else entirely.'

Sabrina examined her slice of toast as if it were the most interesting thing in the world. 'Thing is... I've never been all that comfortable with the dating scene.'

'But you're always going on dates.' Max's frown was one of confusion. 'You've nearly always got someone with you when you go to family gatherings.'

So, he'd noticed that too, had he? Interesting. Sabrina shrugged. 'So? I didn't want everyone to think I was a freak.' She hadn't intended to tell him about her past. It hadn't seemed necessary the night they'd made love. Max's magical touch had dissolved all of her fears of physical intimacy. Well, most of them. But it wasn't physical intimacy that was her problem now. Emotional intimacy was the issue. What if she developed feelings for him that weren't reciprocated? Real feelings. Lasting feelings. *Love* feelings.

'When was the last time you had sex with a guy?' His voice had a raw quality to it.

She looked at the toast in her hand rather than meet his gaze. 'Other than with you? Ten years.'

'Ten years?' The words all but exploded from his mouth.

Sabrina could feel her colour rising. 'I'm sure that seems like a long time to someone like you, who has sex every ten minutes, but I had a bad experience and it put me off.'

He took the toast out of her hand and held her hand in both of his. 'Sabrina...' His thumbs began a gentle stroking of her wrist, his eyes meshing with hers. 'The bad experience you mentioned...'

His throat rose and fell as if he was trying to swallow a boulder. 'Were you—?'

'No, it was completely consensual,' Sabrina said. 'I was eighteen and fancied myself in love and felt ready to have sex for the first time. I never wanted my first time to be outside the context of a loving relationship. But my so-called boyfriend had another agenda. He just wanted to crow to his friends about getting it on with me. I overheard him telling his friends I was hopeless in bed. The gossip and rumours did the rounds of my friendship group. It was humiliating and I wanted to die from shame. Up until you, I hadn't been brave enough to sleep with anyone else.' She chanced a glance at him from beneath her lowered lashes. 'Go on, say it. Tell me I'm a frigid freak.'

His frown carved a deep V into his forehead, his hands so soft around hers it was as if he were cradling a baby bird. 'No...' His voice had that raw edge again. 'You're no such thing. That guy was a jerk to do that to you. You're gorgeous, sensual and so responsive I can barely keep my hands off you.'

His words were like a healing balm to her wounded self-esteem. So what if he didn't love her? He desired her and that would have to be enough for now. His gentle touch made her body ache to have him even closer, skin on skin. She leaned in and pressed a soft-as-air kiss to his mouth, just a brush of her lips against his. 'Thank you...'

Get Up To 4 Free Books!

Dear Reader,

IT'S A FACT: if you answer 4 quick questions, we'll send you 4 FREE REWARDS from each series you try!

Try **Harlequin® Desire** books featuring heroes who have it all: wealth, status, incredible good looks…everything but the right woman.

Try **Harlequin Presents® Larger-print** books featuring a sensational and sophisticated world of international romance where sinfully tempting heroes ignite passion.

Or **TRY BOTH!**

I'm not kidding you. As a leading publisher of women's fiction, we value your opinions… and your time. That's why we are prepared to reward you handsomely for completing our mini-survey. In fact, we have 4 Free Rewards for you, including 2 free books and 2 free gifts from each series you try!

Thank you for participating in our survey,

Pam Powers

To get your 4 FREE REWARDS:
Complete the survey below and return the insert today to receive up to 4 FREE BOOKS and FREE GIFTS guaranteed!

"4 for 4" MINI-SURVEY

1 Is reading one of your favorite hobbies?
☐ YES   ☐ NO

2 Do you prefer to read instead of watch TV?
☐ YES   ☐ NO

3 Do you read newspapers and magazines?
☐ YES   ☐ NO

4 Do you enjoy trying new book series with FREE BOOKS?
☐ YES   ☐ NO

Please send me my Free Rewards, consisting of **2 Free Books from each series I select** and **Free Mystery Gifts**. I understand that I am under no obligation to buy anything, as explained on the back of this card.

❏ **Harlequin® Desire** (225/326 HDL GNW7)
❏ **Harlequin Presents® Larger-print** (176/376 HDL GNW7)
❏ **Try Both** (225/326/176/376 HDL GNML)

FIRST NAME	LAST NAME

ADDRESS

APT.#	CITY

STATE/PROV.	ZIP/POSTAL CODE

His mouth flickered as if her light kiss had set off an electric current in his lips. He drew her closer, one of his hands going to the back of her head, the other to glide along the curve of her cheek, his mouth coming down to within a breath of hers. But then he suddenly pulled back to frown at her again. 'But that night we made love... My God, I probably hurt you. Did I?'

Sabrina wound her arms around his neck, sending her fingers into the thickness of his hair. 'Of course you didn't. You were amazingly gentle.'

'But you were practically a virgin.' His expression was etched with tension. 'I should have taken more time. I shouldn't have made love to you more than once. Were you sore? Did I do anything you didn't like?'

She shook her head. 'No, Max. I enjoyed every second of our lovemaking. I just wish...' She bit her lip and lowered her gaze.

'Wish what?'

'Nothing. I'm being silly.'

Max inched up her chin with the end of his finger. 'Tell me.'

Sabrina took a breath. 'I've only had sex four times in my life, one time I don't want to even think about any more. The other three times were so amazing that I sometimes wonder if I imagined how amazing they were.'

'What are you saying?'

'I'm asking you to make love to me again.'

His eyes searched hers. 'Is that really what you want?'

She looked into his smouldering eyes. 'I want you. You want me too...don't you?'

His hand slid under the curtain of her hair. 'It scares me how much I want you. But I don't want to complicate things between us.'

'How will it complicate things if we sleep together? It's not as if I'm going to get pregnant.' Her attempt at humour fell flat if his reaction was anything to go by.

He closed his eyes in a slow blink, then he removed her hand from him and stood up. 'I'm sorry, Sabrina, but I can't. It wouldn't be fair to you.' He scraped a hand through his still-damp-from-a-shower hair. 'You're not thinking straight. It's probably baby brain or something.'

'Baby brain?' Sabrina choked out a humourless laugh. 'Is that what you think? Really? Don't you remember how amazing that night in Venice was?'

'Sabrina.' His stern schoolmaster tone was another blow to her flagging self-esteem.

She pushed the tea tray off her legs and set it on the other side of the bed. 'Or maybe sex is always that amazing for you. Maybe you can't even distinguish that night from the numerous other hook-ups you've had since.' She threw him a glance. 'How many have there been, Max?' Tears smarted in her eyes but she couldn't seem to stop herself from throwing the questions at him, questions she didn't really want answered. 'Is that why you've refused to sleep me with since that night? How many have you had since then? One or two a week? More?'

He drew in a long breath and then released it. 'None.'

'None?'

He came and sat beside her legs on the bed and took her hand again, his fingers warm and strong around hers. 'None.'

Sabrina used the back of her free hand to swipe at her tears. 'Are you just saying that to make me feel better?'

'It's the truth. There hasn't been anyone because…' He looked down at her hand in the cage of his, a frown pulling at his forehead.

'Because?'

His gaze met hers and a wry smile flickered across his mouth. 'I'm not sure.'

Sabrina moistened her dry lips. 'Was it…amazing for you too? That night in Venice, I mean?'

He gave her hand a squeeze. 'How can you doubt it? You were there. You saw what you did to me.'

She lowered her gaze and looked at their joined hands, thinking of their joined bodies and the sounds of their cries of pleasure that night. His deep groans and whole-body shudders. 'It's not like I have much experience to draw on…'

He brought up her chin with the end of his finger. 'It was amazing for me, sweetheart. You were everything a man could ask for in a lover.' His frown came back, deeper than before. 'I just wish I'd known you were so inexperienced. Are you sure I didn't hurt you?'

Sabrina placed her other hand on top of his. 'Max, listen to me. You didn't hurt me.'

He brought her hand up to his mouth, pressing his lips against the back of her knuckles, his gaze locked on hers. 'When I saw you at my mother's party last night I was considering offering you more than a one-night fling.' He lowered her hand to rest it against his chest. 'I would've been breaking all of my rules about relationships in doing so, but I couldn't get you out of my mind. Or stop thinking about how good we were together.'

'Then why won't you make love to me again?'

His irises were a deep smoky grey, his pupils wide and ink black, and they flicked to her mouth and back to her gaze. 'You're making this so difficult for me.' His voice was gravel rough and he leaned closer until his lips were just above hers. 'So very difficult...' And then his mouth came down and set hers aflame.

It was a soft kiss at first, slow and languorous, his lips rediscovering the contours of her mouth. But it soon changed when his tongue stroked across her bottom lip. She opened to him and his tongue met hers, his groan of satisfaction as breathless as her own. His hands came up to cradle her face, his fingers splaying across her cheeks, his mouth working its mesmerising magic on hers. The movement of his tongue against hers set off fireworks in her blood. Her pulse raced, her heart thumped, her need for him rising in a hot tide of longing that left no part of her body unaffected. Her breasts tingled at the close contact as he drew her closer, the satin of her nightgown sliding sensually over her flesh.

He lifted his mouth to blaze a hot trail of kisses along her neck to the scaffold of her left clavicle. 'God, I want you so damn much…' His voice came out as a growl, the warmth in his lips as hot as fire. He was making her burn for him. She could feel it smouldering between her legs, the slow burn of lust that he had awakened in her.

'I want you too.' She breathed the words against his lips, her tongue stroking his lower lip, tasting him, teasing him.

He sealed her mouth with his, massaging her lips in a tantalising motion that made her pulse and ache with feverish desire. His tongue danced with hers, an erotic choreography that made her senses sing. One of his hands slipped the shoestring strap of her nightgown down her shoulder, uncovering her right breast. He brought his mouth down to its rosy peak, his caress so gentle it made her shiver with delight. His teeth lightly grazed her nipple, his tongue rolling over and around it until she gave a gasp of pleasure. He lowered the other strap off her left shoulder, the satin nightgown slithering down to her waist, revealing her body to his feasting gaze.

'You are so damn beautiful.'

Sabrina began to lift his T-shirt, desperate to touch his warm male skin. 'I want to touch you.'

He pulled back to haul his T-shirt over his head, tossing it to the floor. He stood and came over to remove the tea tray from the bed and set it on top of a chest of drawers. He came back to her. 'Are you sure about this?'

'Never surer.' Sabrina wriggled out of her nightgown, a part of her a little shocked at her lack of shyness. But hadn't he already seen all there was to see? She loved the way he looked at her with eyes blazing with lust. It was the most ego-boosting thing to see him struggle to keep control. No one had ever made her feel as beautiful as he did. No one had ever made her feel proud to be a woman, proud of her curves, proud of her sounds as desire shuddered through her.

Max swallowed and stared at her for a long moment, seemingly still struggling with the tug-of-war between his body and his brain. Sabrina drank in the sight of him naked, his taut and tanned torso cut and carved with well-defined muscles that would have made Michelangelo drool and sharpen his chisel. She had never thought of a man as being beautiful before—it was a term usually applied to women. But in Max's case it was entirely appropriate. There was a classical beauty about the structure of his face and body, the aristocratic lines and planes and contours reminding her of heroes—both fictional and historical—from times past.

Max gathered her close, his touch as gentle as if he were handling priceless porcelain. It made her skin lift and shiver in a shower of goose-bumps. 'Are you cold?' He frowned and glided his hand over her thigh.

Sabrina smiled and brushed her hand down the wall of his chest, suddenly feeling shy about touching him. But she ached to touch him. To caress him. 'I'm not cold. I'm just enjoying being touched. You have such incredible hands.'

He brought his mouth back to hers in a lingering kiss that made her need of him throb deep in her core. Every movement of his lips, every touch of his tongue, every contact point of his body with hers made her desire build to the point of pain. There was a storm gathering in her feminine flesh, a tight turbulence that spread from her core to each of her limbs like all her nerves were on fire. There was a deep throbbing ache between her legs and every time his tongue flicked against hers, it triggered another pulse of lust that made it throb all the more. She moved against him restively, wanting more but not sure how to ask for it.

Perhaps he sensed her shyness, for he took one of her hands and brought it down between their bodies. 'You can touch me.' His voice was so deep and husky it made her skin tingle to think she was having such an effect on him.

Sabrina stroked him with her fingers, enjoying the satin-wrapped steel of his male flesh. He drew in a sharp breath as if her touch thrilled him as much as his thrilled her. 'Am I doing it right?'

'Everything you're doing is perfect.' His breathing increased its pace, his eyes dark and glittering with need.

She moved her hand up and down his shaft, enjoying the feel of him without the barrier of a condom. Skin on skin. The smoothness and strength of him making everything that was female in her do cartwheels of delight.

After a moment, he removed her hand and pressed her down so he was balanced above her on his elbows. 'I don't want to rush you.'

'Rush me?' Sabrina gave a soft laugh. 'I'm practically dying here I want you so much.'

His slow smile made her heart trip and kick. 'Slow is better. It makes it more enjoyable for both of us.'

She reached down to stroke him again. 'Isn't it killing you to hold on so long?'

His jaw worked as if he was reining in his response to her touch. 'I want this to be good for you. Better than good.'

Sabrina's heart was asking for more room inside her chest. He was the dream lover, the lover she had fantasised about for most of her adult life. A lover who put her needs ahead of his own. A lover who respected her and made sure she enjoyed every second of their lovemaking.

But she wanted more. More of him. All of him. He moved over her, gathering her close, nudging her entrance with his erection, taking his time to move, waiting for her to get used to him before going further.

It was so different from her first time as a teenager. So very different it made her chest tighten with emotion. If only *he* had been her first lover. Her body responded to him like fuel to fire. It erupted into sensations, fiery, pulsating sensations that rippled through her entire body. She welcomed him into her with a breathless gasp of pleasure, her inner muscles wrapping tightly around him, moving with him as he began to slowly thrust. Her need built and built within her, his rhythmic movements triggering electrifying sensations that made every cell of her body vibrate. Tension gathered again in her core, a teasing tantalising tension that was more powerful than before. It was taking over her body, taking over her mind, pulling her into one point of exquisite feeling…

But she couldn't quite complete the journey. Her body was poised on a vertiginous precipice, needing, *aching* to fall but unable to fly.

Max brought his hand down to her tender flesh, caressing, providing that blessed friction she needed to finally break free. And fly she did, in waves and ripples and pulses that left no part of her body unaffected. It was like being tossed into a whirlpool, her senses scattering as shockwave after shockwave rocketed through her. Sabrina heard someone gasping and crying in a breathless voice and realised with a jolt that those primal and earthy sounds had come from her.

Max waited until her storm had eased before he increased his pace, bringing himself to his own release with a series of shuddering movements that made her wonder if he had been as affected by their lovemaking as she. Or was this normal for him? Was sex simply sex for him and nothing else? The physical satiation of primal needs that could be met with any willing female? Or had he been as moved as she had been by the flow and ebb of sensations that were still lingering in her body like waves gently washing against a shore?

He began to play with her hair, running his fingers through the tousled strands, the slight pull on her scalp sending a frisson down her spine. How could one person's touch be so powerful? Evoke such incredible sensations in her body?

After a long moment, he raised his head to look down at her, his hand now cradling the back of her head. His expression was confusing to read, it was as if he had pulled down an emotional screen on his face but it hadn't gone all the way down, leaving a gap where a narrow beam of light shone through. The contours of his mouth that hinted at a smile, the smoky grey-blue of his eyes, the pleated brow that wasn't quite a frown made her wonder if he—like her—was privately a little shocked at how good they were together. 'You were wonderful.' His voice had that gravel and honey thing going on. 'Truly wonderful.'

Sabrina let out a shuddery sigh—just thinking about the sensations he had caused made her shiver in delight. 'Is it like that for you all the time?'

He didn't answer for a moment and she wished she hadn't gone fishing for compliments. Stupid. Stupid. Stupid. Of course it wasn't different for him. Of course it wasn't special. Of course it wasn't unique.

She wasn't special.

She wasn't unique.

Max's hand cupped the side of her face, his gaze more blue than grey—a dark, intense blue that made her think of a midnight sky. 'It's not often as good as that. Rarely, in fact.'

Sabrina's heart lifted like it was attached to helium balloons. 'But it sometimes is?' Why couldn't she just let it drop? But she had to know. She longed to know if he felt even a portion of what she'd felt. Her body would never be the same. How could it? It had experienced a maelstrom of sensations that even now were lingering in her flesh in tiny tingles and fizzes.

A small frown appeared on his brow and his eyes moved between each of hers in a back and forth motion as if he were searching for something he didn't really want to find. 'Sabrina…' He released a short sigh. 'Let's not make this any more complicated than it already is.'

Sabrina knew she was wading into the deep end but couldn't seem to stop herself. 'What's complicated about asking you if the sex we just had was run-of-the-mill for you?'

He held her gaze for a beat and then pushed himself away. He got off the bed and rubbed a hand over the back of his neck, tilting his head from side to side as if to ease a knot of tension.

He let out another sigh and turned back to face her, a twisted smile ghosting his mouth. 'Okay, you win. It was great sex. Awesome. The best I've had in years, which was why I was going to offer you a longer fling yesterday at my mother's party.'

Sabrina searched his expression, wondering whether to believe him or not. How silly was she to push for a confession from him only to doubt it when he gave it to her? 'Do you mean it?' Her voice was as soft as a whispered secret, uncertain and desperately seeking reassurance.

Max came back to sit on the bed beside her. He took one of her hands and brought it up to his mouth, kissing each of her fingertips in turn, his eyes holding hers. 'You're a beautiful and sexy woman. I can't remember a time when I've enjoyed sex more.' He gave another rueful twist of his mouth. 'Maybe I've been dating the wrong type of woman.'

Sabrina lowered her gaze and chewed one side of her mouth. 'Better than not dating at all, I suppose…' She didn't want to think about him dating other women. Now that they'd made love again, it made her sick to think of him kissing and caressing someone else. Thank God he hadn't been with anyone since their night in Venice, but how would she feel if he had? But if she didn't marry him, he would be at liberty to sleep with whomever she wished.

It was her call.

Max tipped up her chin with his finger, meshing his gaze with hers. 'What happened to you when you were eighteen would be enough to put most people off dating for a decade. But you have no need to feel insecure. You're one hell of a sexy partner, sweetheart. That night we first kissed? I wanted you so badly it was all I could do to tear myself away.'

'Really?'

His smile made something in her chest ping. He leaned down to press a soft kiss to her mouth. 'Couldn't you tell?'

Sabrina smiled against his mouth. 'It was kind of an enthusiastic kiss now that I think about it.'

He kissed her again, a longer kiss this time, the movement of his lips stirring her senses into overdrive. He lifted his mouth just above hers, his eyes sexily hooded. 'Is that enthusiastic enough for you?'

She traced the line of his mouth with her finger, her body tingling with excitement at the way his hard body was pressing against her. 'Getting there.'

He captured her finger with his teeth, holding it in a soft bite, his eyes pulsating with lust. 'I want you.'

Sabrina shivered in anticipation and looped her arms around his neck. 'I want you too.'

He brought his mouth back down to hers, kissing her long and deep, his tongue gliding into her mouth with a slow thrust that made her body tremble. His hands cradled her face, his upper body pressing down on her breasts, the skin-on-skin contact thrilling her senses all over again. She could feel the swollen ridge of his erection against her lower body, and her inner core responding with tight contractions and clenches. The sweet tension was building, all her pleasure points in heightened awareness of his touch. One of his hands went to her breast in a slow caress that made her skin tighten and tingle. His thumb rolled over her nipple, back and forth until it was a hard pebble of pleasure. The sensations travelled from her breasts to her belly and below as if transmitted by a sensual network of nerves, each one triggered and tantalised by his spine-tingling touch. He went lower to caress her intimately, his clever fingers wreaking havoc on her senses, driving up her need until she was breathless with it.

But he coaxed her only so far, leaving her hanging in that torturous zone that made her wild with longing. Wild and wanton and racked with primitive urges she'd had no idea she possessed. She felt like she would *die* if he didn't let her come. The need was like a pressure cooker inside her flesh. Building. Building. Building.

He gently pressed her down with his weight, his body entering hers with a smooth deep thrust that made her gasp and groan in delight. Her body welcomed him, worshipped him, wrapped around him in tight coils of need that sent pulses of pleasure ricocheting through her flesh.

He set a slow rhythm at first, but then he gradually increased his pace and she went with him, holding him, stroking his back and shoulders, her body so finely tuned to his that she was aware of every breath he took, every sound he made, every movement of his body within hers.

He rolled her so she was lying on top of him, his hands gripping her hips, encouraging her to move with him in an erotic rhythm that intensified her pleasure. She should have felt exposed and vulnerable but she didn't, instead she felt sexy and desirable. His eyes gleamed with delight as she rode him, naked flesh to naked flesh, hers soft and yielding, his hard and commanding.

Sabrina could feel the tight tingle in the core of her being; the slow build was now a rush of heady sensation threatening to consume her like a swamping wave. It was terrifying and yet tantalising as her body swept her up into a tumult of powerful pulses of pleasure, blissful, frightening pleasure that stole her breath and blanked out her thoughts. She heard herself cry out, a high wail that sounded almost primitive, but she was beyond caring. Her body was riding out a cataclysmic storm that made every pore of her skin tingle and tighten as the waves of orgasm washed over her.

Max continued to move within her, his hands holding her by the hips now, his face screwed up in intense pleasure as he pumped his way to paradise. It was as thrilling as the orgasm she'd just had to watch him shudder through his. The way his hands tightened on her almost to the point of pain, the clench of the toned muscles of his abdomen, the momentary pause before he allowed himself to fly. The raw sexiness of his response made her feel proud of her femininity in a way she had never before.

He arched his head back on the pillow and let out a ragged-sounding sigh as his whole body relaxed. He ran a light hand up and down her right arm, his touch like an electrical current on her sensitised-by-sex skin.

His eyes meshed with hers, holding them in a lock that communicated on another level—a level she could feel deep in her flesh. Their bodies were still connected, neither of them had moved. She hadn't been able to. Hadn't wanted to.

He gave a crooked smile and gathered her close so she was sprawled across his chest. She laid her head against the thud of his heart, and sighed as his hand went to the back of her head in a slow-moving caress that made every hair on her scalp shiver at the roots.

Words didn't seem necessary, although Sabrina had plenty she wanted to say. But she kept her mouth closed. He might hold her like a romantic lover but this was not a love match. She had to keep her head. She had to keep her heart out of this. She closed her eyes and nestled against him, breathing in the musky scent of their coupling. For so long Max had been her enemy. The man she actively avoided or if she couldn't avoid him, she fought with him. But how would she be able to conceal her body's involuntary response to him? How would she stop herself from betraying how he made her feel?

Max wasn't her ideal husband. How could he be when he'd always made it clear he didn't want children? He'd been prepared to marry his ex-fiancée but only on the proviso that the marriage would be childless. He didn't want the things Sabrina wanted, the things she'd wanted since she was a little girl. But now circumstances had forced them together because he refused to walk away from her and their child.

Max moved so he was lying beside her and leaning on one elbow. His free hand moved from her face in a slow caress down between her breasts to rest against the flat plane of her belly. There was a faintly disturbing gravitas about his expression that made her wonder if he was already regretting making love to her. Regretting the child they had made.

Sabrina searched his tense features, noted the shadows behind his eyes. 'Does your decision never to have children have something to do with what happened to your brother Daniel?' She knew she was crossing a line by bringing up the subject of his baby brother. Some of the tiny muscles on his face flinched as if she'd slapped him with the pain of the past.

His hand fell away from her belly and he rolled away and got off the bed, his back turned towards her. 'I was the last person to see him alive.' The words were delivered in a hollow tone that echoed with sadness. 'You didn't know that, did you?' His glance over his shoulder was almost accusing.

Sabrina pressed her lips together and shook her head. 'No…no, I didn't…'

He turned back around and drew in a savage-sounding breath, releasing it in a gust. 'No. Because my parents wanted to protect me from blame.' Guilt was etched on his features and shadowing his gaze in smoky clouds.

She frowned in confusion. Why was he blaming himself for his baby brother's death? 'But Daniel died of SIDS, didn't he?'

'Yes, but I can't help blaming myself.' His throat rose and fell. 'I was seven years old. Surely that's old enough to know if something was wrong with my baby brother? But I must have missed it. I thought he was asleep. If only I had acted earlier, called Mum to check on him or something.'

Sabrina thought of Max as a young child, confused and distraught by the death of his baby brother. Even adults blamed themselves, particularly mothers, when a baby tragically died of Sudden Infant Death Syndrome, so how much more would Max shoulder the blame from his immature and somewhat ignorant perspective as a young child?

'But, Max, you were so young. You shouldn't be blaming yourself for Daniel's death. It was a tragic thing but no way was it your fault. Your parents don't blame you, surely?' She had heard nothing of this from his parents or her own, who were such close friends of Gillian and Bryce Firbank.

'No, of course they don't,' Max said in the same grim tone. 'They were in shock and grieving terribly at the time but they were always careful to make sure I was shielded from any sense of responsibility for Daniel's death. But I couldn't stop blaming myself. Still can't, to be perfectly honest.' He gave a twisted movement of his mouth that was as sad to see as the shadows in his eyes.

'Oh, Max…' Sabrina got off the bed and went to him, put her arms around him and hugged him close. After a moment, she leaned back to look up into his eyes. 'I don't know what to say… I can't bear the thought of you blaming yourself all this time. Have you talked to your parents about it?'

He shook his head, his shoulders going down on a sigh. 'We hardly ever mention Daniel's name now. It upsets Mum too much.'

'Understandable, I guess.'

Max's arms fell away from around her body

and he stepped back, his expression difficult to read. 'My mother had several miscarriages before and after Daniel died. That's why there was such a gap between Daniel and me. She desperately wanted another child after he died, but each time another pregnancy ended, I saw another piece of her fade away.' Something flickered in his gaze. 'I've always felt guilty about my decision not to have children. My parents would love grandchildren. But I realised I can't tell them about this baby of ours until we're through the danger period. It would destroy them to have their hopes raised and then dashed.'

'Your poor mum. I'm not sure I knew about the miscarriages,' Sabrina said. 'Mum's never mentioned it. Neither has your mum.'

'She doesn't talk about it. Hasn't for decades. She's always so upbeat and positive but I know she must still think about it.' He sighed again. 'And that's another thing I blame myself for. My parents' marriage has been tested way too much because of my failure to protect my brother.'

'But your parents are happy together, aren't they? I mean, they always look like they are. Your dad adores your mum and she adores him.'

His mouth gave a twisted movement, his eyes shadowed. 'But how much happier would they have been if I hadn't let them down?'

Sabrina placed her hand on his arm. 'Max, you

haven't let them down. It's not your fault. They're amazingly proud of you. They love you.'

He covered her hand with his and attempted a smile. 'You're a sweet girl, Sabrina. But I have a habit of letting people down in the end. That's why I keep my relationships simple. But nothing about us is simple now, is it? We've made a baby.'

Sabrina hadn't realised until now how deeply sensitive Max was. He was aware of the pain his mother had suffered and was doing all he could to protect Sabrina during the early days of her pregnancy. But marrying him was a big step. Sleeping with him six weeks ago had changed her life in more ways than she had thought possible. 'Max… this offer of yours to marry me…'

His hands came up to cradle her face, his eyes moving back and forth from her gaze to her mouth. His breathing had altered, so too had hers. Their breaths mingled in the small space between their mouths, weaving an intoxicating spell on her senses. 'Maybe I need to work a little harder to convince you, hmm?'

His mouth came down and covered hers, his lips moving in soft massaging movements that made every bone in her body feel like it had been dissolved. She swayed against him, dizzy with need, her body on fire with every spine-tingling stroke and glide of his tongue. The dance of their mouths was like sophisticated choreography, no one else could have kissed her with such exquisite expertise. No one else could have made her mouth feel so alive, so vibrantly, feverishly alive. Her heart picked up its pace, sending blood in a fiery rush to all the erogenous zones of her body, making her acutely aware of pleasure spots that ached to be touched, longed to be caressed. Longed to be filled with his intimate invasion.

Max lifted his mouth off hers, his eyes still gleaming with arousal. 'That one night was never going to be enough. We both know that.'

'Then why didn't you contact me afterwards?'

His mouth shifted in a rueful manner. 'We agreed to stay clear of each other but there wasn't a day that went past that I didn't regret agreeing to that rule.'

Sabrina hadn't been too enamoured with that rule either. Every day of those six weeks she'd ached to see him. Ached to touch him. Ached to give herself to him. But that was how she'd got in to this mess in the first place. Max and she had made a child together from their one night of passion.

Passion but not love.

Max didn't love her and was only offering to marry her because of their child. Her dreams of a romantic happily ever after with a man who adored her were fast disappearing.

'Do you regret this?' Sabrina couldn't hold

back the question. 'Taking our relationship to this level?'

His frown deepened and his hand stilled on her hair. 'No.' He released a jagged sigh and added, 'But I don't want you to get hurt. I'm offering you marriage. Not quite the sort you're after but it's all I can offer.'

Sabrina aimed her gaze at his Adam's apple. 'I know what you're offering, Max… I'm just not sure I can accept it…'

He brought her chin up with his finger and did that back and forth thing again with his eyes, searching hers for any trace of ambiguity. 'We're good together, Sabrina. You know that. We can make a go of this. We've both come from stable backgrounds so we know it'll be the best thing for our child to have both its parents together.'

She felt torn because there was nothing she wanted more than to give her baby a stable up-bringing like the ones she and Max had experienced. Didn't every mother want that for her baby? But would marrying a man who didn't love her be enough in the long run? He might come to love their child, but would he ever come to love her as well? And why was she even asking such a question? She wasn't in love with Max. *Was she?* She had to keep her feelings out of it. If she fell for him it would make her even more vulnerable than she already was.

But she couldn't ignore the chemistry between them when her body was still tingling from head to foot from his lovemaking. Neither could she ignore the dread that if she refused to marry him, he would be free to go back to his playboy life. Sure, he would be an involved father but not permanently on site like hers had been. Sabrina released a sigh and rested her hand against his thudding heart.

'Okay, I will marry you, but we can't tell anyone until after the twelve-week mark. We'll have to keep our relationship secret from our families until then, because no way am I going to be subject to pressure and well-meaning but unsolicited advice from our families.'

The frown relaxed slightly on his forehead but it seemed to lurk in the grey shadows of his eyes. He brushed back her hair from her face and pressed a soft kiss to her lips. 'They won't hear about it from me.'

CHAPTER EIGHT

TWO WEEKS PASSED and Sabrina's noisy and cramped flat became a distant memory. All of her things had now been moved and were either in storage or at Max's house. She was touched by his attention to detail, the way he made sure everything was perfectly set up for her. Nothing seemed too much trouble for him, but she couldn't help wondering if he was finding the rapid change in his neat and ordered life a little confronting.

But for her, living with him showed her how seriously she had misjudged him in the past. It made it harder and harder to remember exactly why she had hated him so much. Or had that been a defence mechanism on her part? Somehow her heart had recognised that he was the one man who could make her fall for him and fall hard.

Each time Holly came in for a fitting, Sabrina had to quell her own feelings of disappointment that her wedding wasn't going to be as she had dreamed and planned for most of her life.

But Holly wasn't Sabrina's best friend for nothing and it didn't take her long to pick up on Sabrina's mood at her fitting that afternoon. 'You don't seem yourself today, Sabrina. Is something wrong?'

Sabrina placed another pin in the skirt of Holly's gown to mark where she needed to take it in. 'Other than my husband-to-be is only marrying me out of duty because I'm pregnant with his baby?'

'Oh, honey,' Holly sighed. 'Do you really think Max doesn't care about you? Personally, I think he's been in love with you for months.'

Sabrina sat back on her heels and looked up at her friend. 'What makes you think that?'

Holly lifted one shoulder. 'It's just a vibe I got when I saw him at that party a few months ago. He was acting all dog-in-the-manger when you were dancing with that other guy.'

'So? He was probably just annoyed with me for drawing attention to myself.' Sabrina picked up another pin. 'Turn a little to the left. That's it.' She inserted the pin at Holly's waistline. 'Have you been dieting? This is the third time I've had to take this dress in.'

Holly laughed. 'Wedding nerves. Or excitement more like.'

There was a silence broken only by the rustle of fabric as Sabrina fiddled with the alterations on the dress.

'Have you and Max set a date for the wedding?' Holly asked.

Sabrina scrambled to her feet and stabbed the pins back in her pincushion. 'Not yet...' she sighed. 'I can't see him wanting a big one. He's never been one for large gatherings. He missed out on the Firbank party animal gene.'

Holly's look was as probing as a spotlight. 'Have you decided what you feel about him?'

Sabrina made a business of tidying up her dressmaking tools. She had been deliberately avoiding thinking about her feelings for Max. They were confusing and bewildering, to say the least. He was the last person she had thought she would fall in love with, but how could she not lose her heart to such a wonderful man? He was everything she wanted in a life partner. He was stable and strong and dependable. He had good family values, he was hard working and supportive.

Yes, he was nervous about becoming a father, which was understandable given what had happened to his baby brother. But she wished he would open up more to her about his concerns. To let her in to his innermost doubts and fears. She had hated him for so long, loathed and resented him, and yet these days she only had to think of him and her heart would flutter and a warm feeling spread through her body. 'It's complicated...' She glanced at her friend. 'I used to think I hated him but now I wonder if I ever did. Was it like that for you with Zack?'

Holly's toffee-brown eyes melted at the sound of her fiancé's name. 'It was exactly like that. I hated him when I first met him but as soon as he kissed me…' she gave a dreamy smile '…I think that's when I fell completely and hopelessly in love.'

Sabrina knew from earlier conversations with Holly that handsome playboy Zack Knight had fallen in love with Holly the moment he'd met her. With Zack's reputation as a celebrity divorce lawyer and Holly a twice-jilted wedding florist, their romance had been the talk of London. And while Sabrina was thrilled Holly and Zack were so in love and looking forward to their wedding in a few weeks' time, it made her situation all the more heart-wrenching. She longed for Max to love her the way she had come to love him. Her feelings for him—now that she'd acknowledged them—were intense and irreversible.

But would she be happy knowing, deep down, he was only marrying her out of a sense of duty?

Max was still privately congratulating himself on keeping his relationship with Sabrina a secret from his family. There was something deeply intimate about keeping their involvement quiet. The bubble of secrecy made every moment with her intensely special, as if they were the only two people left on the planet. He had never felt that close to anyone else before and it was both terrifying and tempting. Tempting to think it could grow and develop into something he had told himself never to aspire to because he didn't deserve it.

Worried he would somehow jinx it, destroy it.

It was still too early for Sabrina to be showing her pregnancy, but just knowing his baby was nestled inside her womb made him feel things he had never expected to feel. Not just fear, although that was there big-time, but flickers of excitement, anticipation, wonder. He caught himself wondering what their child would look like, who it would take after, what traits or quirks of personality it would inherit. He had even stopped avoiding people with prams and now took covert glances at the babies inside.

And he had gone to London's most famous toyshop and bought two handmade teddy bears—one with a blue ribbon and one wearing a pink tutu, because, for some reason, he couldn't get the idea of a tiny little girl just like Sabrina out of his mind. He was keeping the bears for when he and Sabrina came home from their first ultrasound appointment.

The day of the appointment, Max cleared his diary for the whole day because he was in no fit state to work even though it would only take up half an hour or so. He was barely able to speak on the way to the radiography centre as he was so lost in his tangled thoughts. His stomach pitched and pinched, his heart raced and his pulse rioted. What if there was something wrong with the baby?

He hadn't realised until now how much he cared about that little bunch of cells. The feelings ambushed him, making him wonder if other fathers felt like this. Men were mostly at arm's length from a pregnancy, distant from what was going on in their partner's body as it nurtured and sustained new life. But he felt an overwhelming sense of love for the child that was growing in Sabrina's womb. What was ahead for their child? What sort of person would they become? How could he as its father make sure it had everything it needed for a long and fulfilling and healthy life?

Max sat beside Sabrina in the waiting room, took her hand and rested it on his thigh. 'Nervous?'

She gave a wobbly smile. 'A little. Are you? You've been awfully quiet.'

He squeezed her hand. 'Sorry. I'm still getting my head around everything.'

A flicker of worry passed through her blue gaze and she looked down at their joined hands. 'I'm sorry about all of this… I can't help feeling it's my fault we're in this situation.'

'Sabrina.' He tipped up her chin and locked his eyes with hers. 'It's not your fault. If it's anyone's fault it's mine.'

Max was relieved Sabrina had finally agreed to marry him. He wanted nothing more than to provide a stable and loving home for their child. And it would be a loving relationship, though perhaps not in the most romantic sense. He genuinely cared about Sabrina, she had been a part of his life for so long, and yet it had only been recently that he had found out the more complex layers to her personality.

He had been deeply touched when she'd revealed to him what had happened to her as a teenager. He wished she had told him that night in Venice but she hadn't and he had to accept it. Would he have still made love to her? He couldn't answer that question. The need between them was so strong and seemed to be getting stronger.

Sabrina's name was called and they were led into the examination room. Max continued to hold her hand as the sonographer moved the probe over Sabrina's still flat abdomen. How could a baby—his baby—be growing inside her? It didn't seem real until he saw the image of the foetus come up on the screen. He could barely register what the sonographer was saying. All he could think was that was his child floating around in the amniotic sac that would feed and nurture it until it was born in seven months' time.

His chest suddenly felt tight with emotion, his heart thumping with a combination of dread and wonder. What sort of father would he be? How could he trust that he would always do the right thing by his child? He had never thought this day would occur and yet here he was sitting with his wife-to-be and staring at a 3D image of their baby.

His wife-to-be. Sabrina, his fiancée. The mother of his child.

Sabrina's hand grasped his tighter. 'Isn't it incredible?' Her eyes shone with the same wonder he was feeling. 'That's our baby.'

Max squeezed her hand and smiled. 'It sure is.'

'You have a few more weeks to decide if you want to know the sex,' the sonographer said. 'It's usually pretty clear from about eighteen to twenty weeks.'

'Do you want to know the sex of the baby?' Sabrina asked Max after the scan was completed.

'Do you?'

'I asked you first.'

'I'm not a great one for surprises, as you probably know,' Max said. 'But I'll go with what you decide. It's your call.'

Her teeth did that lip-chewing thing that never failed to make him want to kiss away the teeth marks on her pillow-soft lips. 'I kind of want to know but I kind of don't. Does that make sense?'

He smiled and brought her hand up to his lips, kissing her bent knuckles. 'It makes perfect sense. At least you've got a bit of time to make up your mind.'

She nodded and gave a fleeting smile. 'It's a little scary now that I've seen the baby… I mean, it makes it so…so real, doesn't it?'

Max kept her hand in his. 'You don't have to be afraid, sweetie. I'll be with you every step of the way.'

She looked at the printed photo of their baby that the sonographer had given them. 'I wonder who it will take after? You or me? Or maybe a bit of both of us.'

'As long as it's healthy, that's all that matters,' Max said. And even then things could happen. Bad things. Tragic things. His gut churned at the thought and his heart started tripping and hammering again. Boom. Trip. Boom. Trip. Boom. Trip. Boom.

Sabrina must have sensed his disquiet and placed her other hand over their joined ones. 'You'll be a wonderful father, Max. I know you will.'

He tried to smile but it didn't quite work. 'Come on. Let's get you home so you can rest.'

Sabrina wasn't tired when they got home but she was concerned about Max. He had seemed preoccupied at the appointment and he'd kept looking at the photo of the baby since then with a frown pulling at his brow. Was he thinking of all the things that could go wrong even after a healthy baby was born? There were no words to settle his fears because no one could guarantee that nothing would happen to their baby. Even after gestation and infancy, there was still the treacherous landscape of childhood and adolescence. But worrying about it wouldn't change what fate had decided—or so she kept telling herself.

Max came into the bedroom where she was resting a short time later, carrying two shopping bags. He sat on the edge of the bed and passed them to her. 'For the baby, whatever sex it is.'

Sabrina opened the first bag to find a handmade teddy bear wearing a blue ribbon. 'So you think it's a boy?'

He gave a one-shoulder shrug. 'I'm hedging my bets. Open the other bag.'

She opened the bag and pulled out another teddy bear but this one was wearing a pink tutu. It touched her that Max had already gone shopping for their baby. It made her wonder if his growing feelings for the baby would somehow, one day, include her. 'They're so cute, Max. That was so thoughtful of you.'

He picked up the blue-ribboned teddy bear and balanced it on his knee, his finger absently flicking the ribbon around its neck. 'Both Daniel and I had one of these. Our grandparents gave them to us.' Something drifted over his features like a shadow across the sky. 'Daniel's was buried with him; it sat on the top of his coffin during the service. I'm not sure if Mum kept mine or not. I think she found it hard to look at it once Daniel had died.'

Her heart ached at what Max must have felt at his baby brother's funeral. And she felt deeply moved that he had shared with her a little more about his childhood and the sadness he still carried. Sabrina took the bear out of Max's hands and set it beside the pink-tutu-dressed one by her side. She took his hand in hers and stroked the strong tendons running over the back of his hand. 'I have a feeling this baby is going to bring a lot of joy to both our families, but especially to yours. You'll be a fabulous dad. I just know it.'

He gave a ghost of a smile and lifted her hand up to his mouth, pressing a soft kiss to the backs of her knuckles. 'I wish I had your confidence.' He lowered her hand to his lap and circled one of her knuckles with his thumb, a frown settling between his eyebrows. 'I'll do my best to protect you and the baby. But what if I fail?'

Sabrina grasped his hand, squeezing it. 'You won't fail. Don't even think like that, Max. Everyone feels a bit daunted by the prospect of parenthood. It's normal.'

He gave another fleeting smile but a shadow remained in his gaze. 'That reminds me...' He let go of her hand and pulled a small velvet box out of his trouser pocket. 'I have something else for you.' He handed the box to her. 'Open it. If you don't like it we can change it for something else.'

Sabrina took the box and prised open the lid. Inside was an exquisite diamond ring that glinted as the light caught all its facets. Being in the business she was in, she saw lots of engagement rings but none had been as gorgeous as this one. 'Oh, Max, it's beautiful…' She glanced up at him. 'But it looks frightfully expensive.'

'And why wouldn't I buy you an expensive ring?'

Because you don't love me.

She didn't have to say it out loud. It was loud enough in her conscience to deafen her. She looked back at the ring and carefully took it out of its velvet home.

Max suddenly took the ring from her and lifted her hand and slipped it over her ring finger. 'There. What about that? A perfect fit.'

'How did you guess my size? Or is that another thing my parents have told you over the years?'

He gave a twisted smile. 'They might well have. But, no, this time I guessed.'

Sabrina looked down at the ring winking on her finger. She tried not to think about how different this moment might have been if they were like any other normal couple. A couple who had met and fallen in love the old-fashioned way. 'It's a gorgeous ring, Max. Truly gorgeous.'

A frown appeared on his forehead. 'Would you have preferred to choose one yourself?'

'No. This one's perfect.' She glanced at him again. 'But I'll have to only wear it in secret for another month because if either of our parents see this giant sparkler on my hand—'

'Maybe we should tell them.'

Sabrina frowned. 'But I thought we agreed to keep it quiet until the twelve-week mark?'

He took her hand and toyed with the ring on her finger, his inscrutable gaze meshing with hers. 'I know but we've had the first ultrasound and everything looks healthy so—'

She tugged her hand out of his and held it close to her body. 'No, Max. I think we should wait. It's only another month and then we can tell everyone about the baby and…and set a date for the wedding.' Every time she thought about the wedding she had a panic attack. How was she going to get a dress made in time? What if she ballooned and looked nothing like the picture she had in her mind of the bride she had always wanted to be?

But it wasn't just about looking the part…what if Max *never* came to love her? People who genuinely loved you never deserted you. It was love that sheltered and sustained a relationship, not an overblown sense of duty.

Max captured her hand again and stroked it in warm, soothing motions. 'I don't want you to think

I'm hiding you from my parents out of shame or embarrassment, like we're having some tawdry little affair. I'm proud to be your partner.'

Sabrina squeezed his hand. 'Oh, Max, that's so sweet of you. But I'm kind of enjoying our little secret. I'm surprised we've managed to keep it quiet this long. But I'm sure that's only because my mum and dad are away on holiday at the moment. I told Mum when she phoned me that I was moving out of my flat to stay with a friend. Unusually for her, she didn't ask which one, but it won't be long before she does.'

'But would it be such a problem to tell her you're staying with me? I don't want to come between you and your parents, especially your mother. And especially now you're pregnant.'

Sabrina rolled her eyes. 'You know what my parents are like, always telling me what I should do. I know they mean well, but as soon as they know I'm pregnant they'll whip out their medical bags and whisk me off to have every test under the sun. I just want to have time to get used to it myself. I'm enjoying the secrecy and the privacy for now.'

Max turned her hand over and traced a lazy circle in her palm. 'I'm enjoying it too.'

'You are?'

His eyes glinted. 'So much so, I think we should go away for the weekend.'

A bubble of excitement formed in her chest. 'Where to?'

'It's a secret.'

Sabrina gave him a coy look. 'You kind of like your secrets, don't you?'

He gave a quick grin that transformed his face. 'More than I realised. Can you take the time off work? I know you usually work on a Saturday but—'

'It's fine. My assistant Harriet is getting better all the time so she can take over while I'm away. I figured she's going to have to do more and more for me the further along I get with the pregnancy.'

Max stroked his hand over the back of her head. 'How long will you work? I can support you if you'd like to take more time off and—'

'I love my job, Max. Pregnancy isn't a disease. I'm perfectly healthy and—'

'I just worry about you doing too much. Running a business more or less singlehandedly is not an easy task. You need to outsource so you're not overburdened with unnecessary work. We have a wedding to plan and a baby on the way and that needs to take priority, surely?'

How could he suggest she take time out from the business she loved as if it was nothing more than a fill-in job? Sabrina swung her legs over the edge of the bed and stood. 'Will you stop lecturing me about what I should do? You're starting to sound like my parents.'

'Yeah, well, maybe your parents are onto something.' Max's tone tightened.

She glared at him, stung by his betrayal in siding with her parents. 'What's that supposed to mean?'

He released a rough-sounding breath. 'Look, I don't want to argue with you. I'm just saying you need to do things a little differently. You're a talented designer, no question about that, but you can't possibly make every single dress yourself.'

'I don't make every one myself. I have a small team of seamstresses but I do all the hand-sewing myself because that's my signature touch.'

'Would it help if I set up a workroom for you here?' Max asked. 'You could work from home and get your assistant to run the shop so you can rest when you need to.'

It was a tempting offer. She had often thought of working from home without the distraction of phones and walk-ins who were 'just browsing'. Some of her hand sewing was complicated and painstaking work and she needed to concentrate. And truth be told, she had been feeling a little overwhelmed with it all even before she'd found out she was pregnant. 'You wouldn't mind?'

'Why would I mind?'

'I don't know… I just thought weddings weren't your thing.'

He came back to take her hands in his. 'There is

only one wedding I'm interested in right now and that's ours. And the sooner it happens the better.'

Sabrina chewed the side of her mouth. 'But I need time to make myself a dress.'

'Don't you have one in stock you could use?'

She rolled her eyes and pulled her hands away. 'Duh. I've been planning my wedding since I was four years old. No. I cannot wear a dress from stock. I want to make it myself.'

He frowned. 'How long will it take to make one?'

'I usually have a six-month lead time for most of my clients. I'm only doing Holly's in a shorter time frame because she's my best friend.'

'Six months?' His tone was so shocked she might have well as said it would take a century.

'I might be able to rustle something up a little earlier but I want my dress to be something I can be proud of when I look back on our wedding day.' Not to mention her relationship with Max. But would she look back on that with pride or despair?

'You're stalling.' The note of schoolmaster censure was back in his tone. 'I don't want to wait for months on end to get married. We've made the decision so let's get on with it.'

'I am not stalling,' Sabrina said. 'Weddings are not dinner parties where you invite a few guests, cook some food and open some wine. It takes months of planning and—'

'So we'll hire a wedding planner.'

'Max, you're not listening to me,' Sabrina said. 'I want to plan my own wedding. I want to make my own dress. I don't want it to be a rushed shotgun affair.'

His jaw worked for a moment. 'I'd like to be married before the baby is born. I want it to have my name.'

'The baby will have your name regardless.' Sabrina sighed and came over to him, touching him on the forearm. 'Maybe we can compromise a bit. I can't say I want to walk up the aisle with a big baby bump on show. That's not quite what I envisaged for myself when I was growing up.'

His hands came to rest on the tops of her shoulders, his eyes searching hers. 'Would you be happy with a small and simple wedding, just family and a few close friends?'

She would have to be happy with it because she was starting to realise there wasn't time for her to plan anything else. How far from her childhood dreams had she come? 'Is that what you would like? Something small and intimate?'

One of his hands went to the nape of her neck, the other to cradle the side of her face. 'I'm sorry I can't give you exactly what you want but we can make do.'

Make do. There was that annoying phrase again. But Sabrina was increasingly aware of her habit of idealising stuff and ending up disappointed when nothing met her standards. Maybe it was better this way. To lower her expectations and be pleasantly surprised when it worked out better than she thought. She pasted on a smile. 'Then that's what we'll do. Make do.'

CHAPTER NINE

BY THE TIME the weekend came, Sabrina had almost convinced herself her relationship with Max was just like that of any other young couple in love and preparing for their marriage and a baby. Almost. He whisked her out of London on Friday afternoon, with their weekend bags loaded in the boot of his car, and drove a couple of hours into the countryside to a gorgeous Georgian mansion a few kilometres from a quiet village.

The mansion had been recently renovated for the garden was still showing signs of having had tradesmen's workboots and ladders and other construction paraphernalia all over it. But even in the muted late evening summer light she could see the neglected garden's potential. Roses bloomed in messy abundance, clematis and fragrant honeysuckle climbed rampantly over a stone wall, and along the pathway leading to the front door she could see sweet alyssum filling every crack and crevice in a carpet of white and purple.

'What a gorgeous place,' Sabrina said, glancing at him as helped her out of the car. 'Is it yours?'

'Yes. Do you like it?'

'I love it.' She breathed in the clove-like scent of night stocks and sighed with pleasure. 'Wow. It's just like out of a fairytale. I'm almost expecting fairies or goblins to come dancing out of that back section of the wild garden.'

Max took her hand. 'Come on. I'll show you around.' He led her to the front door, taking care she didn't trip over the cracked pathway. 'I bought it a while back. I've been coming down when I can to do some of the work myself.'

She gave him a sideways glance. 'Well, I know from personal experience how good you are with your hands.'

He grinned back and squeezed her hand. 'Cheeky minx. Careful, the sandstone step here is a bit uneven. I was going to replace it but I quite like the fact it's been worn down over the years.'

It was becoming more and more apparent to Sabrina that Max was a traditionalist at heart. He was always careful in his designs to respect a building's history and incorporate it cleverly into any new development on the same site, just as he had done with his house in Notting Hill. And wasn't his determination to marry her because of the baby another indication of his commitment to his strong values?

Max unlocked the door and led her inside the house, switching on lights as he went. The interior had been tastefully decorated in mostly neutral colours, which brought in more light. The furniture was a mixture of old and new and she wondered if he'd chosen it himself or got an interior decorator to do it for him. He would certainly know plenty in the course of running his architectural firm. Most of whom would be female.

Sabrina swung her gaze back to his. 'You have excellent taste. Or did you get someone to do the decorating for you?'

He kicked at the crooked fringe on the rug on the floor with his foot to straighten it out. 'There's a woman I use now and again. She's good at listening to what I want and getting on with it.'

The big green-eyed monster was back and poking at Sabrina's self-esteem. 'Is that all you use her for?'

Max frowned. 'Pardon?'

Sabrina wished she hadn't spoken. She turned away and ran her hand over a beautiful walnut side table. 'Nothing…'

He came up behind her and placed his hands on her shoulders and turned her to face him. 'Sabrina. Listen to me.' His voice was gentle but firm. 'You and I are in a committed relationship. You don't have to worry that I'll be looking at any other woman. Ever. Understood?'

She chewed at her lower lip. 'I'm sorry but I can't help feeling a little insecure. It's not like we're in love or anything. How can you be so certain you won't fall in love with someone else?'

His hands tightened on her shoulders. 'Stop torturing yourself with unlikely scenarios. I realise this is a tricky time for you. You have crazy hormonal stuff happening and a lot has happened in a short period of time. But believe me when I say I'll remain faithful to our marriage vows. You have my word on that, sweetheart.'

Sabrina looked into his grey-blue eyes and wished there was a magic spell she could cast that would make him fall in love with her. It would be so much easier to relax and enjoy every facet of their relationship if she thought it was founded on the things that were most important to her.

He was offering commitment without love. Other men offered love and then reneged on the commitment. Could she continue to hope and pray Max would find the courage to relax the guard around his heart and love her as she longed to be loved? She stretched her mouth into a smile. 'Thank you.'

He inched up her chin and planted a kiss on her lips. 'Come on. I'll show you upstairs.'

Sabrina followed him up the staircase to the landing, where eight bedrooms each with their own bathroom were situated. The master bedroom was huge with a gorgeous window seat that overlooked the rambling garden and the landscape beyond. Sabrina knelt on the chintz-covered cushioned seat and looked at the wonderful view of rolling fields and the dark green fringe of forest and wondered if she had ever seen such a beautiful setting. 'Gosh, it's so private. Are there any neighbours?'

'Not close by,' Max said. 'That's why I bought it. It's nice to get away from the hustle and bustle every now and again.'

Sabrina rose from the window seat. 'Do you plan to live here one day? It's a big house for one person. I mean, you weren't planning on settling down and all.'

He reached past her to open the window to let in some fresh air. 'It's more of a weekender. I find it relaxing to be surrounded by nature instead of noise. It clears my head so I can work on my designs.'

Sabrina bit her lip and fiddled with the brass knob the curtains were held back by. 'As big as this place is, you might not get much head space when there's a wailing baby in the house…'

He took her hands in his, his thumbs stroking the backs of her hands. 'Are you nervous about being a mum?'

'A little…yeah, actually a lot.' She sighed. 'I know women have been having babies for ever but it's my first baby and I can't help feeling a little worried I won't be good enough.'

He cut back an incredulous laugh and squeezed her hands. 'Not good enough? You'll be the best mum in the world. You're a natural nurturer.'

'But don't you worry about how this baby is going to change both our lives? I mean, a bit over a month ago we were both single and hating each other. Now we're having a baby and getting married.'

'I have never hated you.' His tone had a strong chord of gravitas.

But what did he feel for her? 'You certainly gave me that impression. Not that I can talk, of course.'

His expression was cast in rueful lines. 'Yes, well, with our parents watching us like hawks for any sign of a melting of the ice between us, I guess we both did or said things we regret now.'

Sabrina moved closer as his hands went to her hips. It never ceased to amaze her how neatly they fitted together like two pieces of a puzzle. 'You're being far too gracious, Max. I seem to remember being an absolute cow to you on a number of occasions.'

He dropped a kiss to the tip of her nose and smiled. 'You're forgiven.'

She smiled back, struck again by how much a smile transformed his features. She lifted her hand to his face and traced the contours of his mouth.

'You have such a nice smile. I don't think I ever saw you smile at me before a few weeks ago.'

'Maybe you're teaching me to lighten up a bit.'

'By accidentally falling pregnant? Yeah, like that's the way to do it.'

He brushed her hair back from her forehead. 'What's done is done. We're moving forward now and it won't help either of us to focus on the negatives about how we got together.' He stepped back with a brief flash of a smile. 'I'm going to bring in our things while you settle in. I've brought some supper for us.'

Sabrina sat on the end of the bed once he'd gone, her thoughts in a messy tangle. Was she being too negative about their situation? She was a lot better off than many young women who suddenly found themselves pregnant after a one-night stand. Max was determined to stand by her and support her. He was bending over backwards and turning himself inside out to be the best partner he could be.

She was grateful he was standing by her, but it didn't stop her hoping his concern for her and the baby would grow and develop into lasting love.

When Sabrina came downstairs, Max had unpacked the car and loaded the fridge with the food he had brought. She was touched by how much effort he had put into making their weekend away so stress-free for her. She hadn't had to do anything but pack her overnight bag.

He came back into the sitting room with a glass of fresh orange juice and some nibbles on a plate. 'Here you go. I've just got to warm up the dinner.'

Sabrina took the juice and smiled. 'Who knew you were so domesticated?'

'Who indeed?'

He sat down beside her and slung his arm along the back of the sofa near her shoulders. His fingers played with the loose strands of her hair, making her scalp tingle and her skin lift in a frisson of delight. 'Not too tired?' he asked.

She leaned forward to put her juice on the coffee table in front of the sofa, then sat back to look at him. 'Not too tired for what?'

His eyes did that sexy glinting thing. 'No way am I making love to you until you've had something to eat, young lady.'

Sabrina shifted so she was straddling his lap, her arms going around his neck. 'But what if all I want right now is you?'

He ran his hands down the length of her arms, his touch lighting fires along her flesh. 'Those pregnancy hormones really are going crazy, hey?'

She had a feeling it had nothing to do with her hormones. It had everything to do with him. How he made her feel. 'Could be.' She brought her mouth down to his, meeting his lips in a kiss that sent a river of flame straight to her core. She could feel the pulsing ache of her body pressed so close to the burgeoning heat of his. The surge of his male flesh reminding her of the erotic intimacy to come.

He drew in a harsh breath as if the leash on his self-control had snapped. One of his hands going to the back of her head to keep her mouth crushed to his. His tongue thrust between her lips, meeting hers in a hot sexy tangle that sent another shiver racing down her spine.

Sabrina set to work on undoing the buttons on his shirt, peeling it away from his body so she could touch his warm hard flesh. He slid his hands under her top, the glide of his slightly calloused hands on her naked skin making her ache for his possession. He deftly unclipped her bra and brought his hands around the front of her body to cradle her breasts. His thumbs stroked back and forth over her nipples, turning them into achingly hard peaks that sent fiery shivers to her core.

'God, you're so damn sexy I can hardly control myself.' His voice was deep and sounded like it had been dragged over a rough surface.

'Don't control yourself, then.' Sabrina licked his lower lip, relishing in the way he shuddered at her touch. 'You can do what you want to me if you'll let me do what I want to you, okay?'

He didn't answer but drew in a ragged breath

and brought his mouth back to hers in a long drugging kiss that involved tongues and teeth and lips and mutual desire so ferocious it threatened to engulf them both.

Sabrina wrenched at his belt fastening, finally getting it undone and tugging it through the lugs of his trousers. She tossed it to the floor over her shoulder and it landed in a snake-like slither on the carpeted floor. She wriggled down off his lap, quickly removing the rest of her clothes, a frisson passing over her flesh when she saw his eyes feasting on her. It amazed her how quickly his body responded to hers and how quickly hers responded to his. Even now she could feel the tight pulses and flickers of need deep in the core of her womanhood, the tender flesh swelling in high arousal, the blood pumping through her veins at breakneck speed.

'Take your trousers off.' Sabrina was a little shocked at how forthright she was being. Shocked but thrilled to be discovering her sensual power. For so many years she had doubted herself, felt ashamed and insecure. But with Max she felt powerfully sexy and feminine. There was no room for shame, only room for the celebration of her sensual awakening.

He stood and stepped out of his trousers, his expression a mixture of rampaging desire and caution at what she might do to him. She pushed him back down on the sofa, bending down on her knees in front of his seated form. 'Now I get to play naughty girl with you.'

Max sucked in another breath and put his hands on her shoulders. 'You don't have to do that—'

'I want to.'

'Oh, God…' He groaned as her hands encased him, moving up and down in massaging strokes the way he had taught her. But she wanted more. She wanted to taste him the way he had tasted her.

Sabrina gave him one long stroke with her tongue from base to tip, delighting in the whole-body shudder he gave. It gave her the impetus to keep going, to torture him with her tongue the way he had done to her. She stroked him again with her tongue, back and forth like she was enjoying her favourite ice cream, casting him wicked tempt-ress glances from beneath half-mast lashes. His breathing rate increased, his body grew more and more tense, every muscle and sinew struggling to keep control. Sabrina opened her mouth over him, drawing him in, sucking and stroking until he was groaning in blissful agony.

Max pulled himself away before he came, breathing hard, his eyes glazed with lust. 'Not all the way, sweetheart.'

'Why won't you let me?'

He got to his feet and picked her up in his arms. 'Because I have other plans for you.'

She linked her arms around his neck and shivered in anticipation. 'Ooh, that sounds exciting.'

He gave her a glinting smile and walked up the stairs, carrying her as if she weighed no more than one of the cushions off the sofa. When they got to the master bedroom, he laid her on the bed and came down beside her, his thighs in an erotic tangle with hers. He cupped one of her breasts in his hands, bringing his mouth down to take her tight nipple into his mouth. He swirled his tongue around its pointed tip, then gently drew on her with a light sucking motion that sent arrows of heat to her core. He moved to her other breast, pleasuring her with the gentle scrape of his teeth and the flick and stroke of his tongue.

Sabrina moved restlessly beneath him. 'Please. I want you *so* much…' Her body was throbbing with the need to feel him inside her. The hollow ache between her legs was unbearable, every nerve primed and poised for the erotic friction it craved.

'I want you too, so damn much, I'm nearly crazy with it.' He moved down her body, holding her hips with his hands as he kissed her abdomen from her belly button down to the top of her mound. She drew in a sharp breath as his mouth came to the heart of her desire. He separated her with the stroke of his tongue, moving along her sensitive flesh in a series of cat-like licks that made every hair on her head shiver at the roots.

It was too much and it wasn't quite enough. Her nerves were tight as an over-tuned cello string, vibrating with the need for release. And then she was suddenly there, falling apart under the ministrations of his lips and tongue, shattering into a million pieces as the tumult of sensations swept through her. She cried, she laughed, she bucked and moaned and clutched at his hair, but still he kept at her until the very last aftershock left her body. She flung her head back against the bed, her breathing still hectic. 'Oh, my God…that was incredible.'

Max placed a hand on her belly, a triumphant smile curving his mouth. 'But wait. There's more.' He moved back over her, careful not to crush her with his weight, and entered her with a smooth, thick thrust, making her gasp all over again.

He set a slow rhythm at first, but then he increased the pace at her urging. She wanted him as undone as she had been. She moved her hands up and down the bunched muscles of his arms, then placed them on his taut buttocks, kneading and stroking the toned flesh as his body moved intimately within hers.

'You feel so damn good.' His voice was part moan, part groan as his mouth came back to hers.

Sabrina kissed him back, using her lips and tongue and even her teeth at one point. The intensity of his passion for her was thrilling. The movement of his body, the touch and taste of him delighting her senses into an intoxicating stupor. She arched her spine, desperate to get closer, to trigger the orgasm she could feel building in her body.

He slipped a hand underneath her left hip, lifting her pelvis and shifting slightly to change the contact of their hard-pressed bodies. And just like that she was off again in a heart-stopping release that sent shockwaves through every inch of her flesh. It was like fireworks exploding, fizzing and flickering with blinding light and bursts of colour like a shaken kaleidoscope.

Sabrina was conscious of the exact moment he let go. She felt every shudder, every quake, felt the spill of his essence and held him in the aftermath, listening to the sound of his breathing slowly return to normal. There was something almost sacred about the silence that fell between them. The quiet relaxation of their bodies, the synchronisation of their breathing, the mingling of their sensual fragrances and intimate body secretions was so far removed from her first experience of sex it made her love for Max deepen even further.

Max leaned on one elbow and placed his other hand on her thigh. 'Was that exciting enough for you?'

Sabrina smiled a twisted smile and touched his stubbly jaw in a light caress. 'You know it was.'

He captured her hand and kissed her fingertips, holding her gaze with his. 'I've never been with a more responsive partner. Every time we make love you surprise me.'

She aimed her gaze at his Adam's apple, feeling suddenly emotional. 'I know I've said it before, but I wish you'd been my first lover. I can't believe I let that jerk mess with my head so much and for so long.'

He cradled her close, his hand gently brushed back her hair from her forehead. 'Sweetie, if I were ever to find myself alone with that creep I would delight in giving him a lesson on how to respect women. What he did to you was disgusting and unforgiveable.'

Sabrina couldn't help feeling touched by the flare of righteous anger in his eyes. It was wonderful to have someone stand up for her, someone who respected and cared about her welfare. Even if he didn't love her the way she wanted to be loved, surely it was enough that he would move heaven and earth to take care of her and their baby? 'You're such a good man, Max.'

He pressed a soft kiss to her lips and then lifted himself off the bed. 'Stay here and rest. I'll bring supper up in few minutes.'

Sabrina propped herself up on the elbows. 'Are you sure you don't want some help?'

He pointed a finger at her but there was a smile in his eyes. 'Stay. That's an order.'

She gave him a mock-defiant look. 'You know how obstreperous I get when you issue you with me orders. Are you sure you want to take that risk?'

His eyes ran over her naked form in a lustful rove that made her want him all over again. 'Are you spoiling for a fight, young lady?' His voice was a low deep growl that did strange things to the hairs on the back of her neck.

Sabrina got off the bed and sashayed across to him with a sultry smile. She sent her hand from the top of his sternum to the proud bulge of his erection. 'I was thinking more along the lines of making love, not war. Are you on?'

He shuddered at her touch and pulled her closer. 'I'm on.' And his mouth came down on hers.

CHAPTER TEN

AN HOUR OR so later, Max sat across from Sabrina in the cosy kitchen of the cottage and watched as she devoured the supper of soup and fresh bread and fruit he'd brought with him. He wondered if he would ever get tired of looking at her. Her hair was all tousled where his hands had been in it, her lips were swollen from his kisses and her cheeks had a beautiful creamy glow.

She looked up to see him looking at her and her cheeks went a faint shade of pink. She licked her lips and then, finding a crumb or two, reached for her napkin and dabbed at her mouth. 'What?'

Max smiled and pushed his untouched bread roll towards her. 'I like watching you eat. You remind me of a bird.'

'Yeah? What type? A vulture?' She picked up the bread roll and tore it into pieces. 'Seriously, I can't believe my appetite just now. I'm starving.'

'Must be the hormones.'

She gave him a sheepish look. 'Or the exercise.'

His body was still tingling from said exercise. And that was another thing he wondered if he'd ever tire of—making love with her. 'I should have fed you earlier. It's almost midnight.'

'I love midnight feasts.' She popped another piece of bread in her mouth, chewed and swallowed, and then frowned when she saw his water glass. 'Hey, didn't you bring any wine with you? I'm the one who isn't drinking while I'm pregnant, not you.'

'That hardly seems fair,' Max said. 'I'm not a big drinker in any case.'

'Oh, Max, that's so thoughtful of you. But I don't mind if you have a glass of wine or two.'

'It's not a problem.' He passed her the selection of fruit. 'Here, have one of these peaches.'

After a while, she finished her peach and sat back with a contented sigh. 'That was delicious.'

He got up to clear the table. 'Time for bed?'

She smothered a yawn. 'Not before I help you clear this away.' She pushed back her chair and reached for the plates.

'I'll sort it out. You go up and get comfortable.'

She was halfway to the door when she turned around to look at him with a small frown wrinkling her forehead. 'Max?'

'What's up, sweetie?'

'Have you brought anyone else down here? Another woman, I mean?'

'No. I've only just finished the renovations.' He picked up the plates and cutlery and added, 'I wasn't going to share it with anyone, to be perfectly honest. Even my parents don't know about it.'

'Why haven't you told them?'

'There are some things I like to keep private.'

She chewed at her lip. 'I've been thinking… It must have been hard for Lydia, knowing your parents didn't think she was right for you.'

Funny, but Max could barely recall what his ex-fiancée looked like now. 'Yes, it probably was hard for her.' He frowned and continued. 'I sometimes wonder if I only got engaged to her to stop them banging on about you.'

Something flickered through her gaze. 'Not the best reason to get engaged.'

'No.'

'Have you seen her since?'

'No. What would be the point? We've both moved on.'

She gave him a thoughtful look. 'But have you?'

'Have I what?'

'Moved on.'

Max turned and loaded the dishwasher. 'You can rest easy, Sabrina. I have no lingering feelings for Lydia. You're my priority now.'

'But in a way, it's the same, isn't it?'

He closed the dishwasher with a snap. 'What's the same?'

'The way you felt about her is similar to how you feel about me. You weren't in love with her and you're not in love with me.'

Max didn't like where this conversation was heading. He wasn't incapable of love. He just chose not to love in *that* way. It wasn't called 'falling in love' for nothing. You lost all control when you loved someone to that degree. He was worried that if he fell in love he would eventually let the person down. Hadn't he always done so? His parents? His baby brother? Even Lydia had been short-changed and had gone off looking for someone who could love her the way she wanted.

'Sabrina.' He let out a long sigh. 'Let's not have this discussion this late at night. You're tired and—'

'What are you afraid of?'

He gave a short laugh to lighten the atmosphere. 'I'm not afraid of anything. Now, be a good girl and go upstairs and I'll be up in a second.'

She looked like she was going to argue, but then she let out a sigh and turned and headed upstairs.

Max leaned his hands on the kitchen counter and wondered if this was always going to be a stumbling block in their relationship. But he assured himself that Sabrina wasn't in love with him so what was the problem? If she had been, wouldn't she have said so? No, they were two people forced together because of circumstance and they were both committed to making the best of the situation. They had put their enmity aside, they liked each other, desired each other and respected each other. If that wasn't a positive thing, what was? Their relationship had a lot more going for it than others he'd seen. And it was certainly better than any relationship he'd had in the past.

Way better.

Sabrina spent the rest of the weekend with her mouth firmly closed on the subject of Max's feelings for her. She didn't want to spoil the relaxing time together because she could see how hard he was trying to do everything right by her. Her feelings weren't the top priority right now. They had a baby on the way and she had to somehow reassure Max he would be a wonderful father. She knew it still troubled him and she ached to ease that painful burden for him.

She consoled herself that in time he might relax the guard around his heart, open himself to loving her once he fell in love with their baby. Didn't most new parents say the experience of bringing a child into the world was a defining moment? A time when overwhelming love flooded their beings? It was her hope, her dream and unceasing prayer that Max would feel that groundbreaking love for their child and include her in it.

A few days later, Max left for a brief trip to

Denmark, where he had a project on the go. Sabrina could sense his reluctance to leave her but she assured him she would be fine as she had work aplenty of her own to see to. Most days her nausea was only mild and if she was sensible about getting enough rest she was able to cope with the demands of her job.

Living at his house had far more benefits than she had first realised, not least the warm protective shelter of Max's arms when she went to sleep each night and when she woke each morning. Staying at his house was like living in a luxury hotel but much less impersonal. There were reminders of him everywhere—books, architectural journals he was reading, one with a feature article on him—and even the house itself with its stylish renovation that perfectly married the old with the new.

There was that word again—*marriage*.

But she couldn't bring herself to regret her acceptance of his proposal. She had to concentrate on what was best for the baby and put her own issues aside. Max cared about her otherwise he wouldn't have made such a fuss over her, looking after her, insisting on her living with him and doing a hundred other things for her that no one had ever done for her before.

The evening he was due to come back, Sabrina found a photo of him with his family in the study, taken before his baby brother had died. She had seen the photo at his parents' house in the past but somehow she hadn't really looked at it in any detail before. She traced her finger over Max's bright and happy smile as a seven-year-old boy and wondered if the birth of their baby would heal some of the pain of the past. There was no doubt in her mind that he would make an excellent father.

The sound of the doorbell ringing almost made her drop the photo frame. Max was due home any minute, but surely if it was him he would use his key rather than the doorbell? She placed the photo back on Max's desk and went out to check the security monitor in the foyer to see who was at the door. Her heart nearly jumped out of her chest when she saw it was her mother standing there with Max's mother Gillian. She had thought her mother would be away for another week in France…or had she got the dates wrong?

Sabrina stepped backwards away from the monitor, hoping Gillian Firbank and her mother hadn't heard her footsteps on the black and white tiles of the foyer, but in her haste she stumbled and bumped against the hall table. She watched in horror as the priceless vase that was sitting there wobbled and then crashed to the floor, shattering into pieces.

'Max?' Gillian said, rapping firmly at the door. 'Is that you? Are you okay?'

Sabrina stood surrounded by the detritus of the vase, her heart hammering faster than that of a rabbit on the run. Should she open the door? But how could she explain why she was at Max's house? They were supposed to be keeping their relationship a secret. But if their mothers found her in situ at Max's home...

'Perhaps it's a burglar,' Sabrina's mother said. 'We'd better call the police.'

Sabrina had no choice but to open the door before her mother summoned half of London's constabulary to Max's house. 'Hi,' she said. 'I'm... erm...housesitting for Max.'

Gillian's and Sabrina's mother's eyes widened and then they exchanged a twinkly-eyed glance.

'Housesitting? For...Max?' Her mother's voice rose in a mixture of disbelief and hope.

'Yes. Just while he's in Denmark. He's coming back tonight. In fact, I thought he would be home before this. Perhaps his flight's been delayed.'

Gillian's mouth was tilted in a knowing smile. 'I knew something was going on with you two at my party.'

'Nothing's going on,' Sabrina lied, not very well by the look on the two women's faces.

'I wanted to show your mother Max's new renovations,' Gillian said. 'We were in the area and saw the lights on and thought we'd pop in. But if Max isn't home we'll come back another time.'

'You told me the other day you were staying at a friend's house.' Her mother's expression was one part accusatory, one part delighted.

'Yes, well, that's sort of true,' Sabrina said.

'So you two are friends now?' Her mother's eyes danced like they were auditioning for a part in *La Cage aux Folles*.

'Mum, it's not what you think—'

'Actually, it is what you think,' Max said as he came up the path to the front door carrying his travel bag with his laptop case slung over his shoulder. 'Sabrina and I are getting married.'

'Married?' The mothers spoke in unison, their faces so aglow with unmitigated joy they could have lit up the whole of London.

Max put his arm around Sabrina's waist and drew her close to his side. 'Yes. We haven't set a date yet but we'll get around to it soon.'

Sabrina glanced at him with a question in her eyes but he simply smiled and bent down to kiss her. 'Miss me, darling?' he said.

'You have no idea how much.' Sabrina bit her lip. 'I'm sorry about your vase…'

'What vase?'

She pointed to the shattered pieces of porcelain strewn over the foyer behind them. 'I bumped it when I was checking the security monitor. Please tell me it wasn't valuable.'

'Not as valuable as you,' he said, and kissed her again.

'Oh, look at you two gorgeous things.' Gillian grabbed Sabrina's mother's arm to lead her inside Max's house. 'We need to celebrate. Let's open some champagne.'

Sabrina gave him a *what do we do now?* look, but his expression remained calm. 'They had to find out sooner or later,' he said, sotto voce, and led her inside behind the older women.

Before she knew it, Max had efficiently cleaned up the pieces of the vase and Sabrina found herself sitting beside him on one of the sofas in the main sitting room. Her mother and Gillian were sitting opposite with glasses of champagne raised in a toast.

'Why aren't you drinking yours, Sabrina?' her mother asked after everyone else had sipped theirs. Max had only taken a token sip, however.

Sabrina cradled her glass in her hands, her cheeks feeling so hot she could have stripped the paint off the walls. 'Erm…'

'Oh, my God!' Gillian shot to her feet as if a spring in the sofa had jabbed her. 'You're pregnant?'

Max looked like he was the one suffering morning sickness. Sabrina's mother Ellen looked like she didn't know whether to laugh or cry.

Sabrina decided there was no point denying it.

Besides, she wanted her mother to be one of the first to know and not find out some other way. 'Yes, I am pregnant but only eight weeks. We're not telling everyone until the twelve-week mark.'

There were hugs and kisses and hearty congratulations all round and finally, after promising they would only tell their husbands and Sabrina's brothers about the pregnancy, the mothers left.

Max closed the door on their exit with a sigh. 'I'm sorry. I forgot I told my mother to drop in sometime to see the completed renovations.'

Sabrina frowned. 'But why did you have to tell them we're getting married? Why not just say we're having a fling or something? You know how I feel about this. Now they'll be in full on wedding fever mode, telling everyone our business and—'

'I was thinking about it while I was away,' Max said. 'Trying to keep our involvement a secret is going to cause you more stress than you need right now. I figured it was safer to get this out in the open. I didn't realise my mother would twig about the pregnancy, though.'

Sabrina sank back into the sofa and hugged one of the scatter cushions, eyeing her untouched glass of champagne as if it had personally insulted her. 'If I hadn't broken that damn vase, trying to avoid them, we might still have kept our secret safe. Argh. I hate how out of control my life is right now.'

He hunkered down next to her and grazed his knuckles across her cheek, his eyes warm and tender. 'It was going to come out sooner or later. And there's no reason to think your pregnancy isn't going to continue.'

'Would you prefer it if I lost the baby?'

He flinched. 'No. How can you ask that?'

She shrugged one shoulder and tossed the cushion to one side. 'I've done a pretty good job of stuffing up your neatly controlled life.'

He straightened and then came to sit beside her on the sofa, his hand slipping under the curtain of her hair to the nape of her neck, his expression wry. 'Maybe it needed shaking up a bit.'

Sabrina could feel every inch of her body responding to his touch. She placed her arms around his waist, loving the strength and warmth of his body so close to hers. She rested her head against his chest and sighed. 'At least our families are happy for us.'

He lifted her face off his chest and meshed his gaze with hers. 'It's a good start.'

'But what if we make each other miserable? I mean, further down the track?'

He brushed an imaginary hair away from her face. 'We're both mature adults. We can handle the odd difference of opinion, surely? Besides, I quite like arguing with you.'

A smile tugged at her mouth, a hot tide of

longing pooling in her core. 'Do you fancy a fight now?'

His eyes glinted. 'Bring it on.' And he scooped her up in his arms and carried her to the bedroom.

CHAPTER ELEVEN

A FEW DAYS LATER, Sabrina had left the shop early, leaving Harriet in charge so she could get home to make a special dinner. They had been eating out mostly but she wanted to have a night at home for once. She suspected he took her out for dinner so often so she wouldn't have to cook but she enjoyed cooking and wanted to do something for him for a change.

Max's once-a-week housekeeper had been through the house and left it spotless. Holly had given Sabrina some fresh flowers and she placed them in the new vase she'd bought to replace the one she'd broken.

He came in just as she was stirring the Provençale chicken casserole on the cooktop and she put the spoon down and smiled. How could a man look so traffic-stopping gorgeous after a long day at work? 'How was your day?'

'Long.' He came over and planted a kiss on the top of her head. 'Mmm…something smells nice.'

Sabrina held up the spoon for him to have a taste. 'It's one of your favourites. Your mum told me.'

He tasted the casserole and raised his brows in approval. 'Delicious. But why are you cooking? Shouldn't you be resting as much as possible?'

'I like cooking.'

'I know, but you don't have to wait on me. I could have picked up a takeaway to save you the bother.'

Sabrina popped the lid back on the pot. 'I'm not waiting on you. I just wanted to do something for you for a change. You've been so good about everything and I—'

'Hey.' He placed his hands on her shoulders and turned her so she was facing him. 'I like doing things for you. I want to make this relationship work.'

She bit down on her lip. 'I know. For the baby's sake, right?'

His hands gave her shoulders a gentle squeeze. 'Not just for the baby. For you. I care about you, Sabrina. Surely you know that?'

She gave an on-off smile. Would caring be enough for her? 'I know but—'

He placed a finger over her lips. 'No buts. I care about you and will do everything in my power to make you happy.' He lowered his hand and brought his mouth to hers instead, kissing her leisurely, beguilingly until she melted into his arms.

Sabrina wound her arms around his neck, pressing herself closer to the tempting hard heat of his body. Her inner core already tingling with sensation, his mouth triggering a tumultuous storm in her flesh. His tongue met hers and she made a sound of approval, her senses dazzled by the taste of him, the familiar and yet exotic taste that she craved like a potent drug. His hands cradled her face as he deepened the kiss, his lips and tongue wreaking sensual havoc, ramping up her desire like fuel tossed on a naked flame. It whooshed and whirled and rocketed through her body, making her aware of every point of contact of his body on hers.

With a groan Max lifted his mouth from hers. 'How long can dinner wait?'

Sabrina pulled his head back down. 'Long enough for you to make love to me.'

He kissed her again, deeply and passionately. Then he took her hand and led her upstairs, stopping to kiss her along the way. 'I've been thinking about doing this all day.'

'Me too,' Sabrina said, planting a series of kisses on his lips. 'I'm wild for you.'

He smiled against her mouth. 'Then what's my excuse? I've been wild for you for months.'

He led her to the master bedroom, peeling away her clothes and his with a deftness of movement that made her breathless with excitement. The touch of his warm strong hands on her naked skin made her gasp and whimper, his hands cupping her breasts, his lips and tongue caressing them, teasing her nipples into tight peaks of pleasure. The same tightly budded pleasure that was growing in her core, the most sensitive part of her hungry, aching for the sexy friction of his body.

Max worked his way down her body, gently pushing her back against the mattress so she was lying on her back and open to him. It was shockingly intimate and yet she didn't have time to feel shy. Her orgasm was upon her as soon as his tongue flicked against the heart of her and she came apart in a frenzied rush that travelled through her entire body like an earthquake.

He waited until she came down from the stratosphere to move over her, entering her with a deep but gentle thrust, a husky groan forced from his lips as her body wrapped around him. Sabrina held him to her, riding another storm of sensation, delighting in the rocking motion of his body as he increased his pace. Delighting in the strength and potency of him, delighting in the knowledge that she could do this to him—make him breathless and shuddering with ecstasy.

Max collapsed over her, his breathing hard and uneven against the side of her neck. 'You've rendered me speechless.'

Sabrina stroked her hands over his lower back. 'Same.'

He propped himself up on his elbows, his eyes still dark and glittering with spent passion. 'I mean it, sweetie. I don't think I've ever enjoyed sex as much as I have with you.'

She couldn't imagine making love with anyone but him. The thought appalled her. Sickened her. She snuggled closer, her arms around his middle, wondering if it were possible to feel closer to him than she did right now.

After a long pause he stroked a strand of hair away from her face, his eyes dark with renewed desire. 'How do you think dinner is holding up?'

She rubbed her lower body against his pelvis and smiled her best sexy siren smile. 'It'll keep.' And she lifted her mouth to the descent of his.

Max had a run of projects that urgently needed his attention. He'd been neglecting his work in order to take care of Sabrina, making sure she had everything she needed in the early weeks of her pregnancy. But his work could no longer be postponed. He had big clients who expected the service they paid good money for. He hated leaving Sabrina but he had a business to run and people relying on him.

Travelling out of town meant he would have to stay overnight and that's what he hated the most.

Not waking up next to her. Not having her sexy body curled up in his arms, the sweet smell of her teasing his nostrils until he was almost drunk on it. He informed her of his business trip over breakfast and she looked up from buttering her toast with disappointed eyes. So disappointed it drove a stake through his chest.

Her smile looked forced. 'Oh… Thanks for telling me.'

He scraped a hand through his hair. Clearly he had some work to do on his communication skills. And his timing. 'I'm sorry. I should have told you days ago. I thought I could manage it at a distance but the client is getting restless.'

She got up from the table and took her uneaten toast to the rubbish bin and tossed it in. 'I know you have a business to run. So do I.'

'Why aren't you eating? Do you feel sick?'

She turned from the bin with a combative look her on face. 'I'm fine, Max. Stop fussing.'

He came over to her and took her stiff little hands in his. 'Do you think I really want to leave you? I hate staying in hotels. I would much rather wake up with you beside me.'

Her tight expression softened. 'How long will you be away?'

'Two nights,' Max said, stroking the backs of her hands. 'I'd ask you to come with me but I know you're busy with Holly's dress. Which reminds me, we need to set a wedding date. My mother has been on my back just about every day to—'

'Yeah, mine too.' Her mouth twisted. 'But I don't want to get married close to Holly's wedding day. But neither do I want to be showing too much baby bump on ours. I don't know what to do. Ever since I was a little girl, I've dreamed of my wedding day. Not once in those dreams did I picture myself waddling up the aisle pregnant. I'm stressing about it all the time. Whenever I think about it I just about have a panic attack.'

He cupped her cheek in his hand. 'Oh, sweetie, try not to stress too much. We'll talk some more when I get back, okay?'

She sighed. 'Okay…'

Max kissed her on the forehead, breathing in her summer flowers scent. 'I'll call you tonight.' He touched her downturned mouth with his fingertip. 'Why don't you ask Holly to stay with you while I'm away? I'm sure she wouldn't mind.'

'She spends every spare minute with Zack.' A spark of annoyance lit her gaze. 'Besides, I don't need flipping babysitting.'

'I can't help worrying about you.'

She slipped out of his hold and picked up her tote bag where it was hanging off the back of a chair. 'You worry too much. I'll be fine. I have plenty to keep me occupied.'

Max placed his hands on her shoulders, turning

her to face him. 'You'll have to be patient with me, Sabrina. I'm not the world's best communicator. I'm used to going away for work at a moment's notice. But obviously that's going to have to change once we become parents.'

She let out a soft sigh. 'I'm sorry for being so snippy. I'm just feeling a little overwhelmed.'

He brought up her chin with his finger, meshing his gaze with her cornflower-blue one. 'It's perfectly understandable. We'll get through this, sweetheart. I know we will.'

She gave another fleeting smile but there was a shadow of uncertainty behind her eyes. 'I have to run. I have a dress fitting first thing.'

He pressed a kiss to her lips. 'I'll miss you.'

'I'll miss you too.'

Sabrina was ten minutes late to her fitting with her client, which was embarrassing as it had never happened before. But she couldn't seem to get herself into gear. Ever since she'd found out Max was going away, she'd felt agitated and out of sorts. It wasn't that she wanted to live in his pocket. She had her own commitments and responsibilities, but she had come to look forward to their evenings together each day. She loved discussing the events of the day with him over dinner, or curling up on the sofa watching television. She had even got him hooked on one of her favourite TV series. She loved the companionship of their relationship. It reminded her of her parents' relationship, which, in spite of the passage of years, seemed to get stronger.

And then there was the amazing sex.

Not just amazing sex, but magical lovemaking. Every time they made love, she felt closer to him. Not just physically, but emotionally. It was like their bodies were doing the talking that neither of them had the courage to express out loud. She longed to tell him she loved him, but worried that if she did so he would push her away. She couldn't go through another humiliation of rejection. Not after what had happened when she was eighteen. But even so, she had to be careful not to read too much into Max's attentive behaviour towards her. He cared for her and he cared about their baby.

That was what she had to be grateful for.

Holly came in for her final fitting later that afternoon just on closing time. 'Hiya.' She swept in, carrying a bunch of flowers, but then noticing Sabrina's expression frowned. 'Hey, what's up?'

Sabrina tried to smile. 'Nothing.'

Holly put the flowers down. 'Yeah, right. Come on, fess up.'

Sabrina was glad Harriet had left for the day. She closed the shop front door and turned the 'Closed' sign to face the street. 'Come out the back and I'll do your fitting while we chat.'

'Forget about the fitting—we can do that another day,' Holly said, once they were out the back. 'The wedding isn't for another few weeks. What's wrong?'

Sabrina put her hand on her belly. Was it her imagination or had she just felt a cramp? 'I'm just feeling a bit all over the place.'

'Are you feeling unwell?'

'Sort of...' She winced as another cramp gripped her abdomen.

Holly's eyes widened. 'Maybe you should sit down. Here...' She pulled out a chair. 'Do you feel faint?'

Sabrina ignored the chair and headed straight to the bathroom. 'I need to pee.'

She closed the bathroom door, taking a breath to calm herself. Tummy troubles were part and parcel of the first weeks of pregnancy. Nausea, vomiting, constipation—they were a result of the shifting hormones. But when she checked her underwear, her heart juddered to a halt. The unmistakable spots of blood signalled something was wrong. She tried to stifle a gasp of despair as a giant wave of emotion swamped her.

Was she about to lose the baby?

Holly knocked on the bathroom door. 'Sabrina? Are you okay?'

Sabrina came out a short time later. 'I think I need to go to hospital.'

* * *

Max was in a meeting with his client when he felt his phone vibrating in his pocket. Normally he would have ignored it—clients didn't always appreciate their time with him being interrupted. Especially this client, by far the most difficult and pedantic he had ever had on his books. But when he excused himself and pulled out his phone, he didn't recognise the number. He slipped the phone back into his pocket, figuring whoever it was could call back or leave a message. But he only had just sat back down with his client when his phone pinged with a text message. He pulled the phone out again and read the text.

Max, it's Holly. Can you call me ASAP?

Max's chest gave a painful spasm, his heart leaping and lodging in his throat until he could scarcely draw breath. There could only be one reason Sabrina's friend was calling him. Something must be wrong. Terribly wrong. He pushed back his chair and mumbled another apology to his client and strode out of the room. He dialled the number on the screen and pinched the bridge of his nose to contain his emotions. 'Come on, come on, come on. Pick up.'

'Max?'

'What's happened?' Max was gripping the

phone so tightly he was sure it would splinter into a hundred pieces. 'Is Sabrina okay?'

'She's fine. She's had a slight show of blood but nothing since so that's good—'

Guilt rained down on him like hailstones. He should never have left her. This was *his* fault. She'd been out of sorts this morning and he'd made it a whole lot worse by springing his trip on her without warning. What sort of job was he doing of looking after her when the first time he turned his back she ended up in hospital? Was there something wrong with him? Was there a curse on all his relationships, especially the most important one of all? His guts churned at the thought of her losing the baby. Of *him* losing her. Dread froze his scalp and churned his guts and turned his legs to water.

'Are you sure she's okay? Can I speak to her?'

'She's still with the doctor but I'll get her to call you when she's finished. She didn't want to worry you but I thought you should know.'

Damn right he should know. But he still shouldn't have left her. He had let her down and now he had to live with his old friend, guilt. 'Thanks for calling. I'll be back as soon as I can.'

'You're free to go home now, Sabrina,' the doctor said, stripping off her gloves. 'The cervix looks fine and the scan shows the placenta is intact. A break-through bleed at this stage, especially one as small as yours, is not unusual. Some women have spotting right through the pregnancy. Just make sure you rest for a day or two and if you have any concerns let us know.'

Sabrina tried to take comfort in what the doctor had said but her emotions were still all over the place. 'I'm not going to lose the baby?'

'I can't guarantee that. But, as I said, things look fine.' The doctor glanced at the engagement ring on Sabrina's hand and smiled. 'Get your fiancé to take extra-special care of you for the next few days.'

Her fiancé...

Sabrina wished Max were waiting outside instead of Holly. Her friend was fabulous and had swung into action as if she had been handling fretting pregnant women all her life. But the person Sabrina most wanted by her side was Max. She felt so alone facing the panic of a possible miscarriage. What if she had lost the baby? What if she *still* lost it? The doctor was right, there were no guarantees. Nature was unpredictable.

Holly swished the curtain aside on the cubicle. 'The doctor said you're fine to go home. Max is on his way.'

'You called him? How did you get his number?'

Holly patted Sabrina's tote bag, which was hanging from Holly's shoulder. 'I found his number on your phone. I didn't feel comfortable calling him on your phone so I called him on mine. I know you didn't want to worry him but if something had happened, imagine how he'd feel?'

Sabrina got off the bed, testing her legs to see if they were as shaky as they had been earlier when panic had flooded her system. 'He would probably feel relieved.'

'What? Do you really think so?'

'I know so.' Sabrina cast her friend a weary glance. 'The only reason we're together is because of the baby.'

Holly frowned. 'But he cares about you. I could hear it in his voice. He was so worried about you and—'

'Worrying about someone doesn't mean you love them,' Sabrina said. 'It means you feel responsible for them.'

'You're splitting hairs. That poor man almost had a heart attack when I told him you were in hospital.'

'I wish I had what you have with Zack,' Sabrina said. 'I wish Max loved me the way Zack loves you. But wishing doesn't make it happen.'

'Oh, honey, I'm sure you're mistaken about Max. You're feeling emotional just now and this has been a huge scare. You might feel better once he's back home with you.'

But what if she didn't?

* * *

Max risked speeding tickets and any number of traffic violations on the way back to London. He'd called Sabrina several times but she must have turned her phone off. He called Holly and she told him Sabrina was back at his house, resting.

'Can you stay with her until I get back?' Max glanced at the dashboard clock. 'I'm about an hour away.'

'Sure.'

'Thanks. You're a gem.' He clicked off the call and tried to get his breathing under control. But every time he thought of what could have happened to Sabrina he felt sick to his guts. Miscarriages were dangerous if help wasn't at hand. It might be the twenty-first century but women could still haemorrhage to death. He couldn't get the picture of a coffin out of his mind. Two coffins. One for Sabrina and another for the baby. How could he have let this happen? How could he have put his work before his responsibilities towards her and their child?

It felt like an entire millennium later by the time Max opened his front door. Holly had obviously been waiting for him as she had her bag over her shoulder and her jacket over her arm.

'She's upstairs,' Holly said.

'Thanks for staying with her.'

'No problem.' She slipped out and Max was halfway up the stairs before the door closed.

Sabrina was standing in front of the windows with her back to him, her arms across her middle. She turned when she heard his footfalls but he couldn't read her expression.

Max wanted to rush over to her and enfold her in his arms but instead it was like concrete had filled his blood and deadened his limbs. He opened and closed his mouth, trying to find his voice, but even that had deserted him. His throat was raw and tight, blocked with emotions he couldn't express.

'You're back.' Her voice was as cold as the cruel icy hand gripping his throat.

'I came as fast as I could. Are you all right?'

She was holding herself almost as stiffly as he was but he couldn't take a step towards her. His legs felt bolted to the floor, his guts still twisting and turning at what might have been.

'I'm fine.'

'And the baby?' He swallowed convulsively. 'It's still—?'

'I'm still pregnant.'

Relief swept through him but still he kept his distance. He didn't trust his legs to work. He didn't trust his spiralling emotions. They were messing with his head, blocking his ability to do and say the things he should be saying. Things he wasn't even able to express to himself, let alone to her. 'Why aren't you in bed? You need to rest.'

A shuttered look came over her eyes. 'Max, we need to talk.'

He went to swallow again but his throat was too dry. Something was squeezing his chest until he could barely breathe. 'You scared the hell out of me. When I got that call from Holly…' His chest tightened another notch. 'I thought… I thought…' In his mind he could see that tiny white coffin again and another bigger one next to it. Flowers everywhere. People crying. He could feel the hammering of his heartbeat in time with the pulse of his guilt.

Your fault. Your fault. Your fault.

'Max, I can't marry you.'

He went to reach for her but she stepped back, her expression rigid with determination. 'You're upset, sweetie. You've had a big shock and you'll feel better once you've—'

'You're not listening to me.' Her voice with its note of gravity made a chill run down his neck.

'Okay.' He took a breath and got himself into some sort of order. 'I'm listening.'

She rolled her lips together until they almost disappeared. 'I can't marry you, Max. What happened today confirmed it for me.'

'For God's sake, do you think I would have left town if I thought you were going to have a miscarriage? What sort of man do you think I am?'

Her expression remained calm. Frighteningly

calm. 'It's not about the miscarriage scare. You could have been right beside me at the hospital and I would still have come to the same decision eventually. You were wrong to force your proposal on me when you can't give your whole self to the relationship.'

'Forced?' Max choked back a humourless laugh. 'You're having my baby so why wouldn't I want you to marry me?'

'But if I had lost the baby, what then?' Her gaze was as penetrating as an industrial drill. 'Would you still want to marry me?'

Max rubbed a hand down his face. He had a headache that was threatening to split his skull in half. Why did she have to do this now? He wasn't over the shock of the last few hours. Adrenaline was still coursing through him in juddering pulses. 'Let's not talk about this now, Sabrina.'

'When will we talk about it? The day of the damn wedding? Is that what you'd prefer me to do? To jilt you like Lydia did?' Her words came at him like bullets. *Bang. Bang. Bang.*

Max released a long, slow breath, fighting to keep his frustration in check. He couldn't talk about this now, not with his head so scrambled, thoughts and fears and memories causing a toxic poison that made it impossible for him to think straight. Impossible for him to access the emotions that went into automatic lockdown just as they had done all those years ago when he'd seen his mother carrying the tiny limp body of his baby brother. It felt like he was a dead man standing. A robot. A lifeless, emotionless robot.

'I put marriage on the table because of the baby. It would be pointless to go ahead with it if you were no longer pregnant.'

Nothing showed on her face but he saw her take a swallow. 'I guess I should be grateful you were honest with me.'

'Sabrina, I'm not the sort of man to say a whole bunch of words I can't back up with actions.'

Tears shone in her eyes. 'You act like you love me. But I can't trust that it's true. I need to hear you say it, but you won't, will you?'

'Are you saying you love me?'

Her bottom lip quivered. 'Of course I love you. But I can't allow myself to be in a one-sided relationship. Not again. Not after what happened when I was eighteen.'

Anger whipped through him like a tornado. 'Please do me the favour of not associating anything I do or say with how that creep treated you. You know I care about you. I only want the best for you and the baby.'

'But that's my point. If there wasn't a baby there wouldn't be an us.' She turned to the walk-in wardrobe.

'Hey, what are you doing?'

'I'm packing a bag.'

Max caught her by the arm. 'No, you're damn well not.'

She shook off his hold, her eyes going hard as if a steel curtain had come down behind her gaze. 'I can't stay with you, Max. Consider our engagement over. I'm not marrying you.'

'You're being ridiculous.' Panic was battering inside his chest like a loose shutter in a windstorm. 'I won't let you walk away.'

She peeled off his fingers one by one. 'You're a good man, Max. A really lovely man. But you have serious issues with love. You hold everyone at a distance. You're scared of losing control of your emotions so you lock them away.'

'Spare me the psychology session.' Max couldn't keep the sarcasm in check. 'I've tried to do everything I can to support you. I've bent over backwards to—'

'I know you have but it's not enough. You don't love me the way I want to be loved. And that's why I can't be with you.'

Max considered saying the words to keep her with him. How hard could it be? Three little words that other people said so casually. But he hadn't told anyone he loved them since he'd told his baby brother, and look how that turned out. He felt chilled to the marrow even thinking about saying those words again. He had let her down and there was nothing he could do to change it. He wasn't good enough for her. He had never been good enough and he'd been a fool to think he ever could be. 'Will you at least stay here for a bit longer till I find you somewhere to live?'

A sad smile pulled at her mouth. 'No, Max, I don't think that would be wise. I'll stay with my parents for bit until I find somewhere suitable.'

Later, Max could barely recall how he'd felt as Sabrina packed an overnight bag and handed him back the engagement ring. He hadn't even said, *No, you keep it*. He'd been incapable of speech. He drove her to her parents' house in a silence so thick he could almost taste it. His emotions were still in an emergency lockdown that made him act like an automaton, stripping every expression off his face, sending his voice into a monotone.

It was only days later, when he got back home to his empty house after work, where the lingering fragrance of her perfume haunted him, that he wondered if he should have done more to convince her to stay. But what? Say words she knew he didn't mean? He would be no better than that lowlife scum who'd hurt her so badly all those years ago.

But why did his house seem so empty without her there? He had got used to the sound of her pottering about. Damn it, he'd even got used to the mindless drivel she watched on television. He would have happily watched a test pattern if he could just sit with his arm around her. He could get through watching just about anything if he could hear the sound of her laughter and her sighs, and patiently hand her his handkerchief when she got teary over the sad bits of a movie.

But he would have to get used to not having her around.

Sabrina dragged herself through the next few days, worn down by sadness that her life wasn't turning out like that of the dewy-faced brides that filed through her shop. It was like having salt rubbed into an open and festering wound to see everyone else experiencing the joy and happiness of preparing for a wedding when her dreams were shattered. Why was her life destined to fall short of her expectations? Was there something wrong with her? Was she too idealistic? Too uncompromising?

But how could she compromise on the issue of love?

Moving back in with her parents might not have been the wisest move, Sabrina decided. She was engulfed by their disappointment as well as her own. It seemed everyone thought Max was the perfect partner for her except Max himself. But she couldn't regret her decision to end their engagement. She couldn't remain in a one-sided relationship. The one who loved the most was always the one who got hurt in the end. She wanted an equal partnership with love flowing like a current between them. Like it flowed between both sets of parents, long and lasting and able to withstand calamity.

No. This was the new normal for her. Alone.

And the sooner she got used to it the better.

A few miserable days later, Max went into his study and sat at his desk. He found himself sitting there every night, unable to face that empty bed upstairs. He sighed and dragged a hand over his face. His skull was permanently tight with a headache and his eyes felt gritty.

His eyes went to the photograph of his family before Daniel had died. There was nothing he could do to bring his brother back. Nothing he could do to repair the heartache he had caused his parents by not being more vigilant. His phone rang and he took it out of his pocket and swore when he saw it was his mother. The gossip network was back at work after a few days' reprieve. No doubt Sabrina's mother Ellen had called his mum to tell her the wedding was off. He was surprised Ellen hadn't done so the moment it had happened but maybe Sabrina had wanted things kept quiet for a bit. He answered the phone. 'Mum, now's not a good time.'

'Oh, Max. Ellen told me Sabrina called off the engagement.'

'Yep. She did.'

'And you let her?'

'She's an adult, Mum. I can't force her to be with me.' Even though he'd damn well given it a good shot.

'Oh, darling, I'm so upset for you and for her,' his mum said. 'I can't help thinking your father, Ellen, Jim and I have been putting too much pressure on you both. We just wanted you to be happy. You're perfect for each other.'

'I'm not perfect for anyone. That's the problem.' He let out a jagged sigh. 'I can't seem to help letting down the people I care about. You, Dad and Daniel, for instance. I do it without even trying. It's like I'm hard-wired to ruin everyone's lives.'

'Max, you haven't ruined anyone's lives,' his mother said after a small silence. 'I know you find it hard to allow people close to you. You weren't like that as a young child, but since we lost Daniel you've stopped being so open with your feelings. It was like a part of you died with him. I blame myself for not being there for you but I was so overwhelmed by my own grief I didn't see what was happening to you until it was too late. But you weren't to blame for what happened, you know that, don't you?'

Max leaned forward to rest one elbow on the

desk and leaned his forehead against his hand. 'I should have known something was wrong. You asked me to check on him and he seemed fine.'

'That's because he *was* fine when you checked on him. Max, the coroner said it was SIDS. Daniel might have died in the next ten minutes and there was nothing you could have done to change that.' She sighed and he heard the catch in her voice. 'Darling, do you think I haven't blamed myself? Not a day goes past that I don't think of him. But it would be an even bigger tragedy if I thought you weren't living a fulfilling life because you didn't think you deserved to love and be loved in return.'

'Look, I know you mean well, Mum, but I can't give Sabrina what she wants. What she deserves. I'm not capable of it.'

'Are you sure about that, Max? Totally sure?'

Max ended the call and sat back in his chair with a thump. It was slowly dawning on him that he had made the biggest blunder of his life. His feelings for Sabrina had always been confusing to him. For years he'd held her at arm's length with wisecracking banter, but hadn't that been because he was too frightened to own up to what was going on in his heart? She had always got under his skin. She had always rattled the cage he had constructed around his heart.

And up until he'd kissed her he'd done a damn fine job of keeping her out. But that one kiss had changed everything. That kiss had led to that night in Venice and many nights since of the most earth-shattering sex of his life. But it wasn't just about amazing sex. There was way more to their relationship than that.

He *felt* different with her.

He felt alive. Awakened.

Hopeful.

His sexual response to her was a physical manifestation of what was going on in his heart. He was inexorably drawn to her warm and generous nature. Every time he touched her, he felt a connection that was unlike any he'd experienced before. Layer by layer, piece by piece, every barricade he'd erected had been sloughed away by her smile, her touch. Her love. How could he let her walk away without telling her the truth? The truth that had been locked away until now. The truth he had shied away from out of fear and cowardice.

He loved her.

He loved her with every fibre of his being. His love for her was the only thing that could protect her. Love was what had kept his family together against impossible odds. Love was what would protect their baby, just as he had been protected. His and her parents were right—he and Sabrina were perfect for each other. And if he didn't exactly feel perfect enough, he would work damn hard on it so he did.

Because he loved her enough to change. To own the feelings he had been too fearful to name. Feelings that he needed to express to her because they were bubbling up inside him like a dam about to break.

Sabrina's parents fussed over her so much each night when she came home from work that she found it claustrophobic. They were doing it with good intentions but she just wanted to be alone to contemplate her future without Max. Thankfully, that night her parents had an important medical function to attend, which left Sabrina to have a pity party all by herself.

The doorbell rang just as she was deciding whether she could be bothered eating the nutritious meal her mother had left for her. She glanced at the security monitor in the kitchen and her heart nearly stopped when she saw Max standing there. But before she allowed herself to get too excited, she took a deep calming breath. He was probably just checking up on her. Making sure she'd settled in okay.

She opened the door with her expression cool and composed. 'Max.' Even so, her voice caught on his name.

'I need to talk to you.' His voice was deep and hoarse, as if he had swallowed the bristly welcome mat.

'Come in.' Sabrina stepped away from the door to allow him to follow but she didn't get far into the foyer before he reached for her, taking her by the hands.

'Sabrina, my darling, I can't believe it has taken me this long to realise what I feel about you.' His hands tightened on hers as if he was worried she would pull away. 'You've been in my life for so long that I was blind or maybe too damn stubborn to see you're exactly what our parents have said all this time. You're perfect for me. Perfect because you've taught me how to feel again. How to love. I love you.'

Sabrina stepped a little closer or maybe he tugged her to him, she wasn't sure. All she knew was hearing him say those words made something in her chest explode with joy like fireworks. She could feel fizzes and tingles running right through her as she saw the look of devotion on his face. 'Oh, Max, do you mean it? You're not just saying it to get me back?'

He wrapped one arm around her like a tight band, the other hand cupped one side of her face, his eyes shining like wet paint. 'I mean it with every breath and bone and blood cell in my body. I love you so much. I've been fighting it because on some level I knew you were the only one who could make me feel love again and I was so worried about letting you down. And then I went and did it in the worst way possible. I can't believe I stood there like a damn robot instead of reaching for you and telling you I loved you that night you came home from hospital. Please marry me, my darling. Marry me and let's raise our baby together.'

She threw her arms around his neck and rose up on tiptoe so she could kiss him. 'Of course I'll marry you. I love you. I think I might have always loved you.'

Max squeezed her so tightly she thought her ribs would crack. He released her slightly to look at her. 'Oh, baby girl, I can't believe I nearly lost you. I've been such a fool, letting you leave like that. How devastated you must have felt when you told me you loved me and I just stood there frozen like a statue.'

Sabrina gazed into his tender eyes. 'You're forgiven, as long as you forgive me for being such a cow to you for all those years.'

He cradled her face with his hands and brushed his thumbs across her cheeks. 'There's nothing to forgive. I enjoyed every one of those insults because they've brought us here. You are the most adorable person in the world. I wish I could be a better man than I am for you, but I give you my word I'll do my best.'

Sabrina blinked back tears of happiness. 'You are the best, Max. The best man for me. The only man I want. You're perfect just the way you are.'

He gave her a lingering kiss, rocking her from side to side in his arms. After a while, he lifted his head to look at her, his eyes moist with his own tears of joy. 'Hang on, I forgot something.' He reached into his trouser pocket and took out her engagement ring and slipped it on her finger. 'There. Back where it belongs.'

Sabrina smiled and looped her arms around his neck again. 'We are both back where we belong. Together. Ready to raise our little baby.'

He hugged her close again, smiling down at her. 'I'm more than ready. I can't wait to be a father. You've taught me that loving someone is the best way of protecting them and I can safely say you and our baby are not going to be short of my love.' He kissed her again and added, 'My forever love.'

EPILOGUE

A FEW WEEKS LATER, Max stood at the end of the aisle at the same church in which he and his baby brother had been christened, and looked out at the sea of smiling faces, his friends and family. He saw Zack sitting with Sabrina's family with a grin from ear to ear, having just got back from his honeymoon. Holly was the maid of honour so Zack would have to do without his new bride by his side while the ceremony was conducted.

Max drew in a breath to settle his nerves of excitement. The church was awash with flowers thanks to Holly. He couldn't believe how hard everyone had worked to get this wedding under way in the short time frame. But wasn't that what friends and family were for? They pulled together and the power of all that love overcame seemingly impossible odds.

The organ began playing 'The Bridal March' and Holly, as Sabrina's only bridesmaid, and the cute little flower girl, the three-year-old daughter of one of Max's friends from University, began their procession.

And then it was time for his bride to appear. Max's heart leapt into his throat and he blinked back a sudden rush of tears. Sabrina was stunning in a beautiful organza gown that floated around her, not quite disguising the tiny bump of their baby. She looked like a fairytale princess and her smile lit up the church and sent a warm spreading glow to his chest.

She was wearing something borrowed and something blue, but when she came to stand in front of him he saw the pink diamond earrings he had bought her after they had found out at the eighteen-week ultrasound they were expecting a baby girl. They had decided to keep it a secret between themselves and it thrilled him to share this private message with her on this most important of days. One day they would tell their little daughter of the magic of how she brought her parents together in a bond of mutual and lasting love.

Sabrina came to stand beside him, her eyes twinkling as bright as the diamonds she was wearing, and the rush of love he felt for her almost knocked him off his feet. He took her hands and smiled. 'You look beautiful.' His voice broke but he didn't care. He wasn't ashamed of feeling emotional. He was proud to stand and own his love for her in front of all these people. In front of the world.

Her eyes shone. 'Oh, Max, I can't believe my dream came true. We're here about to be married.'

He smiled back. 'Our dream wedding.' He gave her hands a little squeeze. 'My dream girl.'

* * * * *

If you enjoyed
The Venetian One-Night Baby
by Melanie Milburne
you're sure to enjoy these other
One Night With Consequences stories!

Consequence of the Tycoon's Revenge
by Trish Morey
The Innocent's Shock Pregnancy
by Carol Marinelli
An Innocent, A Seduction, A Secret
by Abby Green
Carrying the Sheikh's Baby
by Heidi Rice

Available now!

COMING NEXT MONTH FROM

HARLEQUIN

Presents®

Available February 19, 2019

#3697 THE SHEIKH'S SECRET BABY
Secret Heirs of Billionaires
by Sharon Kendrick

Sheikh Zuhal is shocked to discover he has a son! To claim his child, he must get former lover Jazz down the palace aisle. And he's not above using seduction to make her his wife!

#3698 CLAIMED FOR THE GREEK'S CHILD
The Winners' Circle
by Pippa Roscoe

To secure his shock heir, Dimitri must make Anna his wife. But the only thing harder than convincing Anna to be his convenient bride is trying to ignore their red-hot attraction!

#3699 CROWN PRINCE'S BOUGHT BRIDE
Conveniently Wed!
by Maya Blake

To resolve the royal scandal unintentionally triggered by Maddie, Prince Remi makes her his queen! But his innocent new bride awakens a passion he'd thought long buried. And suddenly, their arrangement feels anything but convenient...

#3700 HEIRESS'S PREGNANCY SCANDAL
One Night With Consequences
by Julia James

Francesca is completely swept away by her desire for Italian tycoon Nic! But she believes their relationship can only be temporary—she must return to her aristocratic life. Until she learns she's pregnant with the billionaire's baby!

HPCNM0219RA

#3701 A VIRGIN TO REDEEM THE BILLIONAIRE
by Dani Collins

Billionaire Kaine has just given Gisella a shocking ultimatum: use her spotless reputation to save his own or he'll ruin her family for betraying him! But uncovering sweet Gisella's virginity makes Kaine want her for so much more than revenge...

#3702 CONTRACTED FOR THE SPANIARD'S HEIR
by Cathy Williams

Left to care for his orphaned godson, Luca is completely out of his depth! Until he meets bubbly, innocent Ellie. Contracting her to look after the young child is easy—denying their fierce attraction is infinitely more challenging...

#3703 A WEDDING AT THE ITALIAN'S DEMAND
by Kim Lawrence

To claim his orphaned nephew, Ivo needs to convince the child's legal guardian, Flora, to wear his ring. But whisking Flora to Tuscany as his fake fiancée comes with a complication...their undeniable chemistry!

#3704 SEDUCING HIS CONVENIENT INNOCENT
by Rachael Thomas

Lysandros has never stopped wanting Rio! A fake engagement to please his family is the perfect opportunity to uncover why she walked away... But Rio's heartbreaking revelation changes the stakes. Now he wants to give her everything...

YOU CAN FIND MORE INFORMATION ON UPCOMING HARLEQUIN® TITLES, FREE EXCERPTS AND MORE AT WWW.HARLEQUIN.COM.

HPCNM0219RB

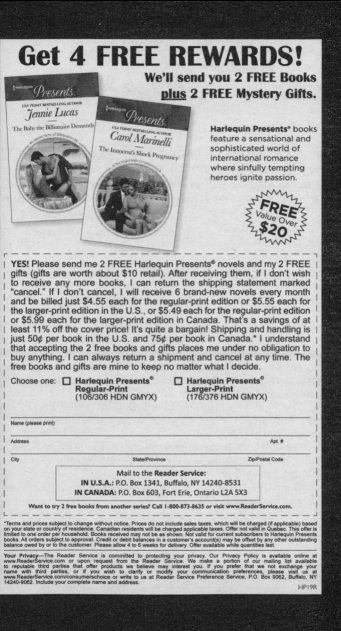

*Ruthless billionaire Kaine has just given Gisella
a shocking ultimatum: use her spotless reputation to
save his own or he'll ruin her family for betraying him!
But uncovering sweet Gisella's virginity makes
Kaine want her for so much more than revenge...*

*Read on for a sneak preview of
Dani Collins's next story,*
A Virgin to Redeem the Billionaire.

"I went to the auction for an earring. I kissed a man who interested me. I've since realized what a mistake that was."

"It was," Kaine agreed. "A big one." He picked up his drink again, adding in a smooth, lethal tone, "I have half a mind to accept Rohan's latest offer just to punish you."

"Don't," Gisella said through gritted teeth, telling herself she shouldn't be shocked at how vindictive and ruthless he was. She'd already seen him in action.

He smirked. "It's amazing how quickly that little sparkler brings you to heel. I'm starting to think it has a Cold War spy transmitter in it that's still active."

"I'm starting to think this sounds like extortion. Why are you being so heavy-handed?"

"So that you understand all that's at stake as we discuss terms."

She shifted, uncomfortable, and folded her arms. "What exactly are you asking me to do, then?"

"You're adorable. I'm not asking. I'm telling you that, starting now, you're going to portray yourself as my latest and most smitten lover." He savored that pronouncement with a sip of wine that he seemed to roll around on his tongue.

"Oh, so you blackmail women into your bed."

For a moment, he didn't move. Neither did she, fearing she'd gone too far. But did he hear himself? As the silence stretched on, she began to feel hemmed in and trapped. Far too close to him. Suffocated.

"The fact you didn't hear the word *portray* says more about your desires than mine," he mocked softly. He was full out laughing in silence at her. So overbearing.

"I won't be blackmailed into playing pretend, either," she stated. "Why would you even want me to?"

He sobered. "If I'm being accused of trying to cheat investors, I want it known that I wasn't acting alone. I'm firmly in bed with the Barsi family."

"No. We can't let people believe we had anything to do with someone accused of fraud." It had taken three generations of honest business to build Barsi on Fifth into its current, iconic status. Rumors of imitations and deceit could tear it down overnight.

"I can't let my reputation deteriorate while I wait for your cousin to reappear and explain himself," Kaine said in an uncompromising tone. "Especially if that explanation still leaves me looking like the one who orchestrated the fraud. I need to start rebuilding my name. And I want an inside track on your family while I do it, keeping an eye on every move you and your family make, especially as it pertains to my interests. If you really believe your cousin is innocent, you'll want to limit the damage he's caused me. Because I make a terrible enemy."

"I've noticed," she bit out.

"Then we have an agreement."

Don't miss
A Virgin to Redeem the Billionaire
available March 2019 wherever
Harlequin Presents® books and ebooks are sold.

www.Harlequin.com

HPEXP0219

HARLEQUIN
Presents®

**Coming next month—
a royal romance with a secret baby twist!**

**In *The Sheikh's Secret Baby* by Sharon Kendrick,
Jasmine is determined that Zuhal will *never* discover
his desert heir. But when he finds out, she has no choice
but to walk down the royal aisle!**

Unexpectedly inheriting the throne is shocking enough.
But when an encounter with former lover Jasmine Jones is
interrupted by the wail of a baby, Sheikh Zuhal also discovers
he has a son! Their secret affair was intensely passionate—and
dangerously overwhelming. To claim his child, Zuhal must get
Jazz down the palace aisle. And he's not above using seduction
to make her his wife!

The Sheikh's Secret Baby

Secret Heirs of Billionaires

Available March 2019

HPBPA0219